CW00859989

Twilight of the Abyss

ISBN: 1449998429

opheliasmuse@gmail.com

Twilight of the Abyss

For Theresa

Chapter One

With a mighty roar, ocean waves crashed upon the rocky beach, the effect of which jarred the foundation beneath Elizabeth's bench. The sun was gone today, and in its place an expansive sky was shrouded with black clouds. From the outside in, she felt the blackness bleeding into her very being, its chill shocking her system.

It was of little matter; she was already numb.

Without thought, she tugged her shawl tighter around herself—it had been scarcely past seven when she had left her sister's for the bench she now rested upon. She reckoned it was now a quarter 'til nine.

They would be wondering where she had gone, but it mattered little. She would return, and they would relax again. It was all a part in a particularly dark play—

feelings were bestowed on an obligatory basis, offered as response from one character to the next. Nothing mattered today that would matter tomorrow. It was all lines to be read. Nothing was real.

In the distance, thunder growled monstrously, and the ocean roiled in answer. Elizabeth watched it all as a conductor, as though it were her own emotions that orchestrated the flare of nature's temper. Again and again the waves slammed against the sand, dragging anything foolish enough to be near the shore back into the current swallowing it whole, drowning the life from it. Wind whipped and stung her cheeks, but Elizabeth did not react. She breathed deeply, as though she had been running, inhaling the salty air, embracing the turmoil. She closed her eyes, and lightning flashed behind the lids.

Like the waves, memories would tumble in and drag her away, enveloping her in an abyss of remove. For a moment, the world would cease spinning on its axis, the sea would calm, and she would just remember…and remember.

The remnants of summer's warmth were finally abating, Elizabeth noted with a sigh, as they arrived at the evening's assembly. Soon the bright green hues of foliage bolstered by sunshine and summer rainstorms would give way to rusty colours of orange and red—and scents of burning leaves and cinnamon would be floating in the crisp air of autumn. She shivered involuntarily, and linked arms with Jane for added warmth.

Mr Bingley appeared at the assembly soon after, with the good humour to please and be pleased with every person he met. As his sisters were cognizant of what it meant to be fashionable, his party did not arrive until the ball was well into its second set. All were very glad to catch a glimpse of Mr Bingley and his party. The ladies were relieved to see that the seven ladies town gossip had fabricated only resulted in two, both of whom were his sisters. The eldest was accompanied by her husband, Mr Hurst, and another gentleman, soon determined to call himself Mr Darcy, was present with them.

Mr Darcy, it was reported, boasted even more wealth than Mr Bingley's five thousand a year. That he was expected to have twice that, and very likely more, infiltrated the minds of gossiping mothers, all anxious of making his acquaintance. Elizabeth had

11

been unable to escape his entrance any less affected, as she found Mr Darcy to be quite handsome. Though Mrs Bennet agreed with her daughter's assessment enthusiastically, Elizabeth suspected that her mother would not find him quite so handsome if he were not quite so rich.

Sir William Lucas, a very amiable gentleman, well-liked for his generous manners and enjoyment of balls and parties, was the man to introduce them. Mrs Bennet collected as many of her daughters as could be located on so short notice and pointed them all out to the gentlemen by name. Elizabeth noted with pleasure that Mr Bingley locked eyes with Jane almost instantly, and had secured her for the next dance before the conversation's end.

Much to Elizabeth's disappointment, her Mr Darcy said very little. However, student of character that she was, she determined that his silence stemmed more from unease than arrogance, and she soon resolved to soothe his discomfort at the first available moment.

As was common, there were several sets that she was obliged to sit out, as there were quite a few more ladies present than gentlemen. She took her seat rather good-naturedly and watched merrily as Mr Bingley danced with Jane another time. Elizabeth could not remember when she had last seen her sister so animated or laughing so often, and she was very glad to see a gentleman appreciate her sister's charms so thoroughly.

As they so often had since their introduction, Elizabeth's eyes sought out Mr Darcy where he stood alone in the shadows for the better part of the evening. This time his gaze caught hers. She dipped her chin, smiling in polite recognition, and was pleased to see him reciprocate similarly. Before more communication between them could be applied, Bingley, who had momentarily removed himself from the dance, came up to his friend.

"Come, Darcy, I must have you dance! I hate to see you standing about in this stupid manner. You had much better dance."

"I certainly shall not," Darcy replied. "You know how I detest it."

"There are several girls here I find to be uncommonly pretty. I should think that many of them would be a vast deal less than a punishment to stand up with."

Darcy pursed his lips, all the while aware of Elizabeth's attention to their conversation. "Your Miss Bennet is very handsome, I grant you. However, I am in no humour to dance, Bingley, you had better go back to your partner."

"Oh, Darcy, she is the most beautiful creature I ever beheld! I do declare she is an angel."

Elizabeth thought she could sense Mr Darcy's amusement with his friend's exultations.

"But look there," Bingley said, indicating to Elizabeth. "There

13

sits her sister. I dare say she is very pretty, too."

Elizabeth lifted her eyes from the hands in her lap she had been fascinated with since the beginning of the gentlemen's conversation. Again, she met eyes with Darcy and cocked her head to the side, brow raised. For her reward, she received a glimpse of a smile before his more solemn expression retrieved it.

"Perhaps you are right," Darcy said more to Elizabeth than Bingley. He stepped closer, and on impulse asked, "Could you be prevailed upon to stand up with me, Miss Elizabeth?" Elizabeth dipped her chin graciously and rose, allowing him to lead her to the dance.

"I am very honoured by your condescension, sir," she began, a smile lingering on her lips, "for I know how you detest this activity."

"You hear uncommonly well."

"Oh, yes, especially when I have the privilege of being seated not three steps away from a conversation!"

Darcy's lips twitched at the sound of her tinkling laughter.

"Though I suspect a gentleman would not be at liberty to express his true feelings aware as he was of perked ears from nearby parties."

"You are quite right," Darcy replied with some amusement, "for I certainly could not refuse to stand up with a lady within earshot."

14

"A capital offence," Elizabeth agreed cheerfully.

"Very ungentlemanly."

"I believe Meryton in general will be very relieved to know that you are not so insufferable as to refuse to dance with its ladies, sir."

"I am glad to prevent such a misunderstanding."

"Indeed," Elizabeth smiled. "Do you intend to stay long with your friends at Netherfield, sir?"

Darcy thought carefully, "My plans are not absolutely set as of yet. Though, I do plan to stay some weeks."

"And from where are you being kept for some weeks?"

"Derbyshire. I have an estate there."

"I do hope you will enjoy your time in Meryton, Mr Darcy. We are nothing to London, I know, but we try our noble best to be hospitable."

"I have no doubts on that count, madam."

"Good," Elizabeth said with a smile. "Though I am disappointed, sir."

"And what has you so cast down, Miss Elizabeth?"

"Well, you see, I do dearly love to laugh, and I find that your manners from the beginning of this dance have been such as to distress me thoroughly."

"Why is that?"

15

"I have found nothing wanting in your addresses, no sourness of expression, no frowns or particular facial contractions. You see, I have nothing over which to tease you, save your time glowering in the corner, and I fear I am obliged to let such behaviour escape my notice in light of such flawless politeness as you have presented just now."

"You cannot know how grieved I am to disappoint, Miss Elizabeth."

"Nor I," she agreed. "I am afraid that there is nothing else for it. We shall have to be friends."

"And you see no other alternative?" Darcy asked with mock gravity.

"No, sir."

Darcy gave her a true smile, his very first of the evening. "Then friends we shall be."

Elizabeth gasped as another clap of thunder snatched her awareness back to the present. Had it truly been above seven months since she had first laid eyes on him? Was that possible? She had come here today with a purpose—to send away all thoughts of what had been. In her hands she held a book of poetry. It was one she had picked up because he had called it his favourite. Even now, after everything that had happened, she had

16

kept it by her side. Today she had meant to cast it into the sea and allow the ocean to wash away her feelings of sorrow and regret. She had tried hating him, she had tried forgetting, but nothing abated the tempest her heart felt at a love that was requited, but not enough.

Absently, she ran her fingertips against the cool, leather binding. Her mind flashed to the destruction it would receive upon hitting the water, though it now rested in her hand undisturbed. Painfully, she realized she could not do it. She could no more destroy the novel than she could forget the man that had inspired her affection for it. She pressed the book to her chest and a tear escaped her eye, but was engulfed by the drizzle that had begun to fall from the heavens. Resolutely, she turned and walked back to the great house. She would conquer this, somehow… and when she needed to cry, she would wait until it was raining outside.

Chapter Two

Saturday, 4 January 1812

Dearest Jane,

I write to you this morning to report I have not seen any evidence of Mr Darcy in London, nor am I likely to. I am not acquainted with his sister, and it is very unlikely that we would ever be invited to the same parties or assemblies. I find myself growing quite indifferent to him. Certainly, if we were to cross one another in the street, I would be perfectly comfortable to carry along my way.

I have known better all along than to expect anything from Mr D. We are too different, the disparity of our circumstances would never permit me to allow such feelings, nor would they permit him to act on any feelings he might have had for me. I know, though, that whatever our acquaintance might have been in Hertfordshire, whatever my fanciful ideas might have entertained, they cannot *survive when practicality must be attended to.*

I am delighted with the news of your engagement to Mr Bingley and beg you to think no more on my situation as I vow I shall not once this letter is sent. Not another blot of ink on this page shall dwell on my unfounded and disappointed hopes.

So Mr Wickham has married Mary King! I cannot say that I am surprised. I suppose his ridding the neighbourhood of himself, and with such a wife, shall be our consolation for having tolerated him as long we did. He may certainly go, and after all the deception he attempted, I doubt any of us will wish him back again.

My aunt has already begun to enquire when she might expect you to travel here for your trousseau. I have assured her that it shall be no menial task to pry you from Mr Bingley's clutches long enough for us to shop!

Mary has written to me. She says she finds herself very comfortable in Kent. Though I never could have been content with such an establishment—with such a husband—I know must I account for our difference in temperament. If she is happy with so silly a man, then I commend her. She has extended an invitation for me to visit Hunsford Parsonage, but I have written back declining the offer just now. I cannot bear the notion of being away from Longbourn any more until you are married. Soon you will be gone and married to your excellent Mr Bingley, and I cannot imagine being away from you for the remainder of your time with us.

I must go now, for my aunt wants me downstairs. Do write soon, dear Jane. I look forward to hearing more of your lovely betrothed. Give my mother and sisters my love and a very special kiss for Papa.

I am,

Your Elizabeth.

Sunday, 5 January 1812

"This is contemptible!" Jane exclaimed, tossing aside Elizabeth's letter and stealing to the window. She rounded on her betrothed, who sat confused on the settee. "She has been led astray! Your friend has acted a part to her all these months only to abandon her now, when he has made her love him!"

Bingley frowned as he mentally worked through all that had happened since they had come to Meryton. "Jane, dearest, Darcy is not the sort of man to torment a young lady. I am convinced within myself that he knew nothing of her feelings when he left for London."

"No, he knew her feelings. He knew, and yet he

20

betrayed her," Jane argued emotionally, tears filling her eyes.

"Jane, my love, do sit down. You are upset. Your compassion will surely come to you."

"My compassion, sir? My compassion is with my sister—the friend I have loved and turned to for every day of my life! That someone could treat her so carelessly is beyond my forgiveness!"

"Will you permit me?" he asked, indicating to the letter. Jane appeared to think carefully before making a decision. "If I permit you to do so, you must understand that I do so with a trust that you will not violate her privacy, nor will you use her thoughts for your own purposes."

"Of course," Bingley replied gravely.

Drying her eyes with a handkerchief, Jane nodded and watched silently as he read her letter. When he was finished, he looked at her with large eyes.

"He cannot know that she is in love. I know Darcy—he is simply incapable of acting so dishonourably. I do not know what has happened, but it *cannot* be so easy as his abandoning her."

Jane's expression softened. "Why would he leave her?"

"I cannot tell you," he sighed, "but I shall get to the bottom of it. He cannot have known her feelings."

"Jane!" Mrs Bennet cried, coming into the room. "Kitty tells me you have had a letter from Lizzy. What news? Has she seen Mr Darcy?"

Without answering, Jane gave her mother the letter. When she was finished, Mrs Bennet seated herself roughly on the cushion. "To go all the way to London and see nothing of Mr Darcy! Mr Bingley, how contemptibly your friend has behaved to our poor Lizzy!"

Jane flushed in embarrassment. "Mama, we do not know the circumstances—"

"Is it not plain enough? How ill he has used her! Her bloom will go as she pines for him, and she will end an old maid! Mark my words, my dear."

"Mother!"

"If I were you, Mr Bingley, I should refuse to ever see Mr Darcy again, for Lizzy is to be your sister, and he has ruined her every hope of happiness. Poor girl, what she must suffer. I doubt we shall know her again when she returns. How altered she shall be!"

Jane was very embarrassed by her mother's speech, and could not look at Mr Bingley, who experienced a great confusion. As he did not know how to behave in the presence of such plainness of speaking, he wisely chose to remain silent. When her mother had left the room to cry to Mr Bennet, Jane looked at her betrothed apologetically.

"She does not mean to be cruel."

Mr Bingley shook his head. "Think nothing of it. She is certainly very upset."

"I wish I could acquit your friend of offence, but I fear I cannot until we know the circumstances."

"You are determined to blame him, I think."

"I am determined to defend my sister," Jane said evenly.

Bingley sighed as he seated himself beside her. His expression was very troubled. "Can you not reserve judgment until we know the particulars?"

Jane's gentle heart could not resist such an entreaty. She placed her hand on his, "Very well. I will try, for *you.*"

"Thank you."

"But only because he is your dearest friend, and not because I think him deserving of any particular consideration."

Bingley sighed. "I fear that this is not the sort of question one may ask outright. If I have the misfortune to offend him, he will tell me nothing."

Jane's mouth set in a line. She was wild to go to her sister in London, yet it was still another week before she was scheduled to travel there for her wedding clothes. She worried that Elizabeth would be beyond conversation by the time she arrived, that she would have resolutely sealed up her feelings on the subject and would allow no one to comfort her. Jane felt for her, as she did not know how she would bear it if she had been similarly abandoned by Mr Bingley. She felt angry and concerned for Elizabeth. They would get to the bottom of this misunderstanding—anything else was indefensible.

Chapter Three

"Papa!"

Elizabeth smiled as the spirited Gardiner children hopped up to greet him. They had been sprawled out in the floor, listening raptly as Elizabeth read to them. She had noticed for some time that their attention had been arrested by the anticipation of Mr Gardiner returning home from work. Every so often, one of them would sit up and peek out the window. Elizabeth could not fault their enthusiasm. They were very fortunate to have such a loving father.

Jane and Elizabeth had always called him "Uncle Sugar-in-His-Pocket" because he always had a treat for them, even if it were nothing more than a spare sugar cube meant for the horses. Mr Gardiner was a very round, jolly man who always had a smile on his face.

25

He and Mrs Gardiner had always been a favourite with the Bennet girls.

Elizabeth had returned with her aunt and uncle after their annual Christmas with the Bennets, a visit originally meant for Jane, but was prevented by her recent engagement to Mr Bingley. Elizabeth had been glad for the change in scenery and relief from her mother's continued expressions of regret over the departure of Mr Darcy. If she were being honest with herself, Elizabeth had cherished a small hope that she would see Mr Darcy in Town—though the likelihood of that was near impossible. She hoped her letter would be enough to put an end to her family's expectations with the gentleman, as she desperately wished to forget the entire endeavour. It had been foolish of her to ever relish the hope that Mr Darcy would look on her as a suitable match. Even if he had entertained that notion, his continued absence in her life spoke testament that she was now long forgotten.

As she returned her attention to the present, she felt a small object land in the palm of her hand. She looked up to see Mr Gardiner standing over her.

"You looked as though you were in need of some lemon candy, Lizzy," he said, giving her a wink.

Elizabeth gave him a genuine smile. "Thank you. I am very glad you are home, Uncle."

Mr Gardiner was prevented from responding by his youngest son running up and attacking his pocket. Elizabeth laughed out loud as the little boy shoved his hand deep into the coat pocket and removed a piece of candy gleefully.

"One day, Lizzy, you will see that your children's behaviour will often depend on what you can give them. I am in luck, however, because I have replenished my resources!" he chuckled, patting his pocket. She watched him go, smiling to himself as he turned the corner. It was one of the many reasons she loved to stay in London, as the Gardiners were always bent upon their home being a happy place.

مۇ

Darcy threw his newspaper in the fire, giving vent to his frustration. The town gossips had fallen over themselves with glee to report his cousin, the Viscount of

27

Rosemont's, marriage to a woman of foundling status—presumed to be a natural child of uncertain parentage—a woman with no connections, no fortune, no education and who had never been in Town until her wedding day.

The marriage had scandalized the Fitzwilliam and Darcy families and had sent Lady Elinor to bed and Lady Catherine into hysterics. His cousin, Colonel Fitzwilliam, had written just that morning that his mother, Lady Elinor, had all but refused to see Gregory and this "wife" when they came to Desham House.

Lady Catherine had written them all very scathing letters, expressing her outraged feelings and her refusal to acknowledge the woman. Darcy could feel how tightly wound the muscles in his shoulders had become. He, too, was astonished at his cousin's behaviour. He had been quick to assume what everyone else had suspected—that Gregory Fitzwilliam, heir to the Desham earldom, had married his mistress—but the man himself insisted that nothing could be further from the truth. The viscount professed himself in love with her. Even so, Darcy was smart enough to recognize the damage that had been rendered to the family name.

Colonel Fitzwilliam had further voiced Darcy's own thoughts by pointing out how damaging this could be for poor Georgiana, who everyone hoped would eventually make a respectable match. There were no misgivings that this charade would have her suitability called into question. The rest of them would have to be very careful in their handling of the affair. Their behaviour would require the strictest adherence to decorum if they ever hoped to put this circumstance behind them.

Chapter Four

Elizabeth and Jane fell into the other's arms as soon as the latter arrived on Gracechurch Street. It had been a full two weeks since Elizabeth's letter had arrived, and both sisters were very glad to be together again. Elizabeth noted the fine blush and freshness adorning Jane's features. There was no doubt she was a woman in love, and Elizabeth was very glad to see it.

"Oh, I am so glad to see you, Lizzy!" Jane exclaimed once they were upstairs. She seated herself close to Elizabeth on the bed they always shared at the Gardiners' house. "And are you well?"

Jane's compassionate gaze confused and embarrassed Elizabeth. She blushed and released her sister's hands. "Of course," she insisted, putting on a brave face. When Jane looked doubtful, Elizabeth rushed to

30

convince her. "I am well, Jane. Truly."

"I cannot believe you have been treated so carelessly."

"Jane! This from you? I did not come to Town to see Mr Darcy. In any case, there is very little chance he is aware of my being here."

"Charles could write to him—"

"No," Elizabeth responded resolutely. "If he sought to know my location, I dare say he could find me easily enough."

Jane looked at her through worried eyes, and Elizabeth pressed her hand to soothe her.

"In any case, Jane, he could have hardly left Hertfordshire with the intention to ever return again— Meryton, as well as the people in it, were undoubtedly a diversion. He has forgotten all about it, I am certain, and I think the surest thing would be for us to follow his example. He will be forgot, and soon I will go on as I did before."

"I am sorry, Lizzy. It was not my intention to upset you."

"I am not distressed, I assure you," Elizabeth replied more cheerfully than she felt. "Now, you must tell me all that has happened since I have been away." Elizabeth relaxed in relief as the topic was turned elsewhere.

اللّٰه

Monday, 20 January, 1812

Darcy,

If you will see me, I should like to pay you a call this afternoon on a matter of import. -Bingley

As he read the note again, Darcy sighed deeply and left his chair to look out the window restlessly. In his quest to exorcise the laughing eyes of Elizabeth Bennet from his mind, Darcy had made a point to communicate little with Bingley after news of his engagement to the lady's sister had reached him. In any case, he and Bingley had not parted well upon his removal to Town. Even now, his initial inclination had been to decline. Darcy had no idea of how their first interaction in months would play out. Now, as he prepared to greet

Bingley, he regretted the rashness of his own temper at the younger man's refusal to take his advice.

"If she is indifferent," Bingley said hotly. "Let her say so herself!"

"Do you truly believe she would be so candid, Charles? Good G-d, do be rational!"

"My feelings for Miss Bennet are not rational."

"Then you are willing to be the object of disappointed hopes, to play the fool when it all comes out that she has married you for your money?"

"If the alternative possibility is that she might marry me because we are in love, then yes, I am willing to take that chance."

"You are a fool, Charles!"

"A fool I may be, but fickle I am not. I have made my preference to her known by everyone. Even if I wished it, to turn my back on her now would expose her to ridicule."

"There is still time for you to quit Netherfield and close

the book on this ridiculous notion."

"A very clever scheme, Darcy, but you forget that I have no desire to silence such hopes and expectations! You dishonour Miss Bennet by presuming she would welcome the attentions of gentlemen for whom she cared nothing."

"A woman has been known to accept a man for less, Charles."

"We are talking now of your own prejudices, are we not, Darcy?"

"I cannot think what you mean."

Bingley narrowed his eyes. "Can you not?"

Bingley sighed with frustration as his friend retreated to the window. In a calmer, more resolute voice, he said, "Go to Town, Darcy. Rid your mind of her, if you must, but I am quite determined. I have no intention of being persuaded otherwise. I am my own man and responsible for my own actions. Though I would be glad to have your approval in all things, I do not require it."

"You are resolved then."

"I am."

"Then I will wish you joy and hope that I am incorrect about Miss Bennet's feelings."

"So do I," Bingley said softly.

"Goodnight." Darcy did not look back as the tapping of his boots echoed down the hallway. Bingley might have been lost, but it was not too late to save himself. He had left with the sunrise the following morning, well on his way before any of his acquaintance had thought to stir. A night of fitful sleep had left him exhausted. He prayed that with some distance, his heart's obsession with the laughing eyes of Elizabeth Bennet would soon dissolve like the morning dew.

Chapter Five

Two months. The next week would mark two months since he had last laid eyes on Elizabeth Bennet. Seven long weeks had passed, and yet his mind continued to habitually turn to her when unoccupied. He dreamed of her, every conversation reminded him of her, and every woman proved their inability to measure up to her. She had become the voice in his head, a spirit that haunted him waking and in sleep. Yet, since his return, events had only further compounded his feelings that a serious attachment to her was unthinkable. She may have been all that was lovely, kind, and intelligent, but he knew he would be the only one who took time to see it once her origins were revealed. Even so, he could not so easily dismiss his guilt for what had passed between them.

"Mr Bingley for you, sir."

Darcy turned from the window to see Stevens let Bingley into the room. He came from around his desk to shake hands with his friend.

"Bingley, it is good to see you."

"Yes, Darcy. I am very glad to see you, too. How have you been?"

"As well as can be, I imagine. Getting on with my usual activities," Darcy said, forcing a pleasant expression as they both took their seats.

Bingley nodded pensively, and Darcy detected a reserve in his friend he was not accustomed to seeing from him. He quickly ascertained that this was not merely a friendly visit.

"Can I get you a drink, Charles?"

"Yes, I think we could both use a brandy."

Darcy nodded and set to his task. "I believe I owe you congratulations, in person, on your engagement."

"Thank you."

"When is the happy day?"

"The third of February. A Monday."

"Soon then!"

Bingley chuckled, "Soon enough for the rest of the world, though for myself it cannot come quickly enough."

Darcy smiled, as he handed Bingley a glass. "Shall you settle at Netherfield?"

"No."

Darcy looked up in surprise.

"I have given up my lease. A retired admiral and his wife intend to take it up after I am gone." Bingley was quiet for several moments before he attempted to explain. "Before he died, my father had been looking closely into the investment of some shipping imports. After a number of conversations with my uncle on the subject, I have decided to move forward with my father's intentions. I have taken an estate off the shore of Yorkshire. Darnwell is its name. We intend to settle there."

"So far?"

"Yes, but we will be close to my family, and it is a very handsome estate. I hope to have you visit me there in the future."

"Of course," Darcy said absently. As he was unused to

Bingley relying upon his own sense for anything, he could not help but be surprised. "I would be glad to visit once you are settled."

Bingley nodded. "I also hope you will stand up with me in February."

Darcy frowned gravely into his glass. The thought of returning to Hertfordshire was unsettling. Bingley, however, was his dearest friend, and he owed him more than that. "It would be an honour."

"Thank you."

There was a silence between them then, as each man became lost in his own thoughts. After several minutes, Bingley spoke.

"Miss Bennet is also here in London. She is staying with her aunt and uncle."

"Is she?"

"Yes, she has come for her wedding clothes. She was very glad to see her sister again," Bingley said carefully, watching the subtle reaction cross Darcy's features.

"Oh?"

"Yes, Miss Elizabeth Bennet has been in town since the week after Christmas. Did you know it?"

"No," Darcy said softly.

"Yes, her sister was thankful to be reunited with her. Apparently, Miss Elizabeth's letters seemed a bit melancholy of late."

Darcy frowned and turned to the window. "I am sorry to hear it."

"As was I."

Darcy turned and almost asked the question that was on his tongue. Almost.

Bingley caught his reaction and continued, "I am hosting a dinner in Miss Bennet's honour, next week. I intend to invite only our families and my closest friends. I hope you will agree to come."

"Of course," Darcy replied uncomfortably, and his voice sounded strained, even to him.

"Good. I will send you an invitation when I know the particulars." He rose and again shook hands with Darcy. "I will keep you from your business no longer. It was good to see you again, Darcy."

Darcy nodded, giving Bingley a small smile. "Indeed it was. Thank you, Charles."

As soon as the man had left, Darcy slumped in his desk

chair and covered his eyes, rubbing them in frustration. A bad situation had just decidedly gotten worse.

Chapter Six

Elizabeth thought it was fearfully warm inside Netherfield as she resolutely stood up with Mr Collins. The heated room had only served to amplify her cousin's less than desirable scent—of wild onions, she had decided. In a misstep, her partner had lost time with the music and slammed squarely into the chest of Colonel Forster. Embarrassed, Elizabeth chewed her lip and looked to where she knew _he_ would be standing. Their eyes locked, and Elizabeth thought she could detect amusement in Mr Darcy's countenance. She puffed her cheeks in frustration as Mr Collins stepped on her foot. An interminable quarter-hour passed, and at last the music ceased. Without waiting to be escorted, Elizabeth bowed to her partner and fled the dance line.

"It was most unkind of you to take pleasure in my suffering," she whispered, coming to stand beside Mr Darcy. "My toes will be *bruised for a week."*

"I see your cousin has set his sights on dancing with your youngest sister."

Elizabeth looked over to see Lydia with a unique expression of misery. Lydia dancing with Mr Collins! She laughed aloud. "What a face she has!"

"Will you do me the honour of standing up with me, Miss Elizabeth? Do you think your toes might bear the experience?"

Pleased, Elizabeth agreed, and as she allowed him to lead her toward the dance, she relished the feeling of her gloved hand resting in his. As they stood closer and began dancing, she caught his familiar scent, one that reminded her of cinnamon and black pepper. She loved dancing with him. Every move Darcy made spoke of his quiet elegance, his graceful masculinity consumed her, and like every other time they had danced, she forgot there was any creature in the word but him.

They always said very little while dancing, both preferring to be mesmerized by the act of giving away and taking their partner back again. Over and back, and through the couples he led her, and Elizabeth, so affected, chose simply to follow. She saw his colour rise and absently acknowledged her colour was high also, yet she could not tear her eyes from his. A connection so deep had passed through them, from one to the other, and Elizabeth was undone.

Too quickly the music stopped and the trance broke. Dizzy, Elizabeth swayed, and would have lost her footing had not two strong hands taken hold of her elbows and steadied her.

"Elizabeth? Are you well?" Darcy asked anxiously.

"I—"

"You are too warm. Come, let us step outside into the fresh air."

Elizabeth felt herself being manoeuvred through the other guests and out into the cool November night. She gasped at the chill. Obviously seeing that she would be too cold, Darcy mindlessly moved closer to cover her bare arms with his large, warm hands. A frisson shot through Elizabeth's body at their closeness. She looked up into his eyes, her heart pounding in her ears. What she saw gazing back at her would change her life forever. In his dark brown eyes, she found a desperation that mirrored her own, an unravelling of feelings never felt before—love. Without knowing what happened, his lips had pressed against hers. The softness of his lips, the gentle pressure of his hands against her arms was beyond any joy she had ever experienced. She exhaled in pleasure against his mouth...

Elizabeth's eyes popped open, and she sat up straight in her bed. Absently, she pressed her cool hands to her burning cheeks. Beside her, Jane slept soundly. She was at her uncle's in London. It had been a dream. She pulled her knees up to her chest in an attempt to ease the aching she felt inside. She was alone. He was never coming back—she had to accept it.

Thinking of his warm, spicy scent and the comfort of his closeness threatened to make her throat close up with emotion. Tears spilling on her cheeks, Elizabeth shook and swallowed the sobs that threatened to make her cry out. Turning, she lay down again and pressed her face into her pillow, crying painfully. He *had* loved her. She had felt it. She had seen it in his eyes. Why had he gone from her? Why?

Chapter Seven

Darcy frowned, his grave expression marring his otherwise handsome features. All along he had assured himself that Elizabeth had not loved him as he had come to love her. He had preferred to believe that her youthful innocence had somehow spared her. But if Bingley was to be believed, she had felt for him, too. Frustrated, he raked his hand through this hair. His kiss had happened so unconsciously that he had been astonished to find his lips pressed against her soft, pink ones. He was a beast that had carelessly left her to hope where there could be none. He had read somewhere that lovers rarely survived without the other. How untrue that was! One survived—but that was almost the extent of such an existence.

Now, to see Elizabeth, to face her after what had happened between them would only further his despair and catapult him deeper into this hellish prison of guilt and pain. The irony of which, was that it was an escape that, as a man of consequence, he was supposed to be thankful for. He did not wish it, but it was what it was. She was considered unsuitable in the eyes of the world, and though a gentleman's daughter, her connections in trade were enough to further humiliate a family still struggling to overcome an even more imprudent match. If it had been only his reputation that answered for Darcy's actions, he could excuse such selfish behaviour on his part. He would have asked Miss Elizabeth to marry him long ago. As it was, he had only gotten out in time, and all the strict demands of propriety and decorum insisted he appreciate his good fortune. However, he could not. He had come to feel deeply for Miss Elizabeth, and his own heart knew how completely he had wronged her.

Their kiss had left him in such a panic that he had practically run from her at Netherfield. It had been the catalyst of his heated confrontation with Bingley and hasty return to Town. Whatever Elizabeth thought of him, he was sure it must be akin to contempt. He deserved her censure, and he rightly deserved her hatred. He had taken her unrehearsed heart and taught it to love, then abandoned her without a word.

But what could he have done? Marriage was not an option, not now, not ever. Elizabeth would find a man who could love her without misgivings or reserve. He would go on with his life—forever regretting his treatment of her. She deserved more than such carelessness, and Darcy dearly wished she would find it. For himself, he thought it only just that he would always regret her. He thought back to when the first seeds of his feelings for Elizabeth had begun to grow. It haunted him how he might have acted differently, yet his own attachment to her had not permitted prudence.

Wednesday, 13 November, 1811

As he rode out that morning, Darcy contemplated his attention to Miss Elizabeth Bennet. So little did he enjoy being amongst strangers, his mood the evening of

48

the assembly had been so foul he had scarcely been capable of feigning civility. However, the moment his eyes met hers, it was as though a light had been lit. Something about her manner had relaxed him. Her eyes, her laugh, her intelligence—he would have to be very careful. If he did not begin to exercise some restraint, he would be in grave danger of raising the lady's expectations. It was thus that for all her smiles and sparkling eyes, Miss Elizabeth was not a suitable match for a man of his station. Her father might have been a gentleman, but her connections combined with the behaviour of her mother and younger sisters were enough to give him pause. No, he could not allow himself to love her—such a match would expose them both to censure and ridicule of the worst kind.

While Darcy was often misconstrued as disagreeable and thinking himself above his company, what was not quickly ascertained was that which lay beneath his impenetrable countenance was a man that felt deeply. He had always considered himself fortunate that he rarely met a woman who caught his eye. In his mind, there had always been the possibility that a young lady with handsome features and little else would eventually come his way. He knew this could be only temptation, as certainly fate would not be so cruel as to snatch his heart along with it.

Throughout his life, it had been impressed upon him the duty he owed both his family and the Darcy name. He would marry a lady of fortune and connections, thus uniting two noble lines and securing the continuation of his own. Alternatives did not exist. Yet, despite his cold and fastidious nature, Darcy was not cruel. He no more wished to see Miss Elizabeth Bennet injured by his lack of self-control than he did himself. Indeed, he had to be very careful.

It came as quite a surprise to him when, upon his return, he was informed that Miss Elizabeth Bennet had arrived to enquire after her sister. He was relieved to learn that she was also upstairs with Miss Bennet at that particular moment. Darcy quickly returned to his chamber, perhaps the one true room at Netherfield where he could be assured he would not encounter her. He seated himself anxiously in a chair by the window while he awaited his valet to attend him.

He was being tested. There was no other explanation for what was happening. He had resolved to behave himself in Miss Elizabeth's company, and now she had been sent to test that resolve. Darcy ran a frustrated hand down his face, feeling the sweat and grime that had accumulated during his ride. He was not a weak man—he had the strength to adhere to his determination—and now was as good as any to act. He would prove to her and himself that the attraction neither of them had any right to presume could be extinguished.

ﻋﻠﻰ

"I would find them just as agreeable had they uncles enough to fill *all* of Cheapside!" Bingley exclaimed passionately.

Darcy scowled into his coffee cup. "With such relations, they have very little chance of marrying well. *That* is the material point, Bingley."

Miss Bingley nodded at her brother pointedly.

"I think you all had better remove the beam from your own eyes before pointing out the speck of mote in the

51

Bennets'. You, my dear sisters, should take care to recall that the fine gowns that drape your figures this evening were purchased with funds rendered from trade. And you, Darcy, I would not be as judgmental as you for a kingdom. If uncles in Cheapside do not give me pause, I daresay there are others that would judge similarly."

"They have other disadvantages to provoke such judgment, Charles," Miss Bingley reasoned. "Their mother? She has no discretion."

"Quite so," Mrs Hurst nodded. "What man would wish to align himself with such a mother-in-law?"

"And I suppose you have determined that although you are *forced* to be amongst such uncouth individuals, you have no duty of common decency to give them your notice or consideration," Bingley said impatiently.

"Did we not invite Miss Bennet for supper?" Miss Bingley replied gently. "You are correct, Charles, she is a dear, sweet girl, and I feel for her. But you must keep your head about you."

Darcy could sense Bingley glowering in his direction, but he did not venture to speak further. He believed himself perfectly justified in his assessment.

"Excuse me, I have quite lost my appetite," Bingley said, and Darcy sighed deeply as he watched his friend toss his napkin on the table and exit the room. A glance at Bingley's sisters was enough to confirm that they were similarly surprised by their brother's outburst. Darcy began to wonder if coming to Netherfield with Bingley had been a mistake.

He stepped into the hall and found Bingley conversing amiably with Miss Elizabeth Bennet on behalf of her sister. Despite his inclination to join their conversation, he thought better of it, and continued on his way. If Bingley would not take care, let it be his own failing, for Darcy was quite determined to remain strong.

Chapter Eight

Elizabeth watched as Darcy dipped his chin without stopping and disappeared into the library. She resisted the inclination to follow him, and tried to attend Mr Bingley. To her embarrassment, she discovered that she had, in fact, no idea what the gentleman had just said. Luckily, she was able to discern by his laugh that Bingley had likely said something he meant to be amusing. Dinner that evening was a sombre affair. The Bingley sisters endeavoured to extend only the smallest appearance of civility to her, and Mr Darcy said nothing at all. Elizabeth soon determined that if Mr Bingley had not attempted to converse with her, she might have passed the meal without above five words being spoken to her.

Cognisant of the fact that she was obviously not a welcome addition to the party at Netherfield, Elizabeth felt embarrassed to have imposed upon their hospitality, even for her sister's sake. Involuntarily, her eyes often sought out Mr Darcy, and each time she found he did not look up from his plate. The coldness from *him* she could not account for, and it startled her how unhappy it made her. Was she so affected by him? Why was he so different? Such was her discontent she excused herself immediately after dinner to return to Jane. She found her sister awake and talkative, which relieved her despite the questioning that came with it.

"Lizzy, will you not tell me what makes you so forlorn?" Jane asked once Elizabeth had gotten a report on her health and had settled down to read aloud from a book.

"I cannot think what you mean."

"You have not smiled since you returned upstairs. Are you so unhappy?"

Elizabeth forced a smile. "It is nothing. Only, I could not help but feel as though I am imposing on the Bingleys by remaining here with you."

"What gave you that impression? What trouble will you be?" Jane demanded. "To make an extra seat at mealtimes and turn down another bed at night? Lizzy, be sensible."

Elizabeth frowned. "You are right, it must have been my imagination."

"I am sure Mr Darcy is very glad to have you here."

Elizabeth raised her brows. "I do not know why you should think he would feel any differently from the rest of our friends here at Netherfield."

"Lizzy, what will it take for you to admit what is obvious to the rest of the world? Mr Darcy has an obvious preference for you."

"I do not know why you suppose that. True, I have offered him compassion instead of judgment, yet one must not think that gives me a particular distinction from the rest. Mr Darcy is a rich man, who convenes within the highest spheres of society. He may be glad to find a friendly face amongst strangers, but beyond that you must not believe."

"Can I not hope for you?"

"No, please, I beg you, do not hope, for there is no

thought of *that.*"

"Has he spoken to you since your arrival?"

Elizabeth set her expression to one of decided reserve. "He has not."

Jane frowned in surprise. The source of Elizabeth's unhappiness soon became clear. "Lizzy, I know he will, though, and soon. He can scarcely take his eyes off of you."

Elizabeth did not reply, instead she opened the book and began reading aloud, silencing further conversation between them.

Darcy was not particularly surprised to find Miss Elizabeth absent from the breakfast table the next morning. The expression on her face the evening before, as she was pointedly ignored by himself and Bingley's sisters, had filled him with a guilt that prevented his sleep that night. He had awakened that morning feeling even less rested than when he had lain down the night before. Darcy's first impulse upon waking had been to locate her and apologise for his behaviour. That she was nowhere to be found was frustrating, though understandable.

He poured himself a cup of coffee and strode toward the window. It was there he spotted her, walking near the edge of the property. Discarding his coffee on the table, he took his gloves and coat and went out after her. He was relieved that Miss Elizabeth slowed her pace when she saw him approaching and accepted his arm when it was offered.

"Good morning, Mr Darcy."

Darcy nodded. "You are out very early."

"I was anxious to take in some fresh air."

"How does your sister fare this morning?"

"She is recovering very well, sir," she replied civilly, then added, "I have hopes that we will not be required to trespass on your friend's hospitality much longer."

Darcy cringed at her reference to their behaviour the previous evening. "You and your sister are always welcome at Netherfield, well or not—though preferably in good health, of course."

"Thank you," she said softly.

The silence of the remaining moments beckoned Darcy

to regret his failing at easy conversation. Eventually, it was Miss Bennet who thought of something to say.

"Do you travel often with Mr Bingley?"

"No, this time would actually be the first. Bingley has great intentions to purchase an estate for himself, and has enlisted my opinion in such matters."

"You must be an invaluable friend."

"Not at all. Bingley is like a brother to me. I am glad to do almost anything for his benefit, as I believe he would for mine."

"His present benefit, I think, is that he reminds you to laugh."

Darcy smiled. "You must be surprised that any person would require it. I doubt you are in need of reminding."

"Oh, Mr Darcy, even the greatest of teasers may forget to let themselves *be* teased from time to time."

"Who reminds you?"

"My family counsels me on a great deal of things. My father makes certain I know how to laugh at myself, Jane reminds me to think well of others, and my mother reminds me never to think myself above my company."

"An invaluable family you have, then."

"They *are* dear to me," she smiled. "And may I ask what your sister reminds you?"

"She reminds me to think well of others, like your Miss Bennet. But it is her presence in my life that reminds me daily of the duty and responsibility I owe her and all my family."

"Such grave reminders," she chuckled lightly. "You are very lucky then to have Mr Bingley to make you laugh!"

Darcy laughed at her teasing. "Indeed."

"But come, sir, surely your sister must be prone to also induce daily happiness!"

At this, Darcy's expression became solemn, and it was some moments before he responded. There was a time when his sister's youthful innocence had lit the halls of their home with laughter. It had once been near impossible to look at Georgiana without smiling. Yet, after suffering a grievous disappointment in the summer, some time had passed since he had seen even the smallest evidence of a smile on her face.

"Georgiana is very shy, Miss Bennet. But you are correct, her happiness is mine."

As Elizabeth watched Jane sleep later that morning, she thought back to the remainder of her walk with Mr Darcy. It concerned her how affected she had become by his presence. In light of his behaviour the day before, she had been rather surprised to have his company for her walk. The opposing sides of his character perplexed her. As she listened to the smooth rhythm of her sister's breathing, she thought back to the things he said of his sister. It had warmed her heart to learn how dear Miss Darcy's happiness was to him.

"She is a very lucky girl to have such a devoted brother," Elizabeth had said seriously.

"On the contrary, Miss Bennet, it is *I* who am very lucky."

Elizabeth could have done nothing but smile at such kind words. Such declarations only served to improve her opinion of him. Darcy was a very good and honourable sort of man. His devotion to his sister spoke volumes of his character. A wealthy man of his situation—unmarried as he was—could afford to accommodate his sister elsewhere in a situation where she would be of very little inconvenience to himself. That he had chosen to keep her at home with him was, in Elizabeth's eyes, the mark of a worthy gentleman. She had regarded his features as they walked, admiring the firm set of his jaw and the colour of his smooth skin. The elegance which he carried his tall frame commanded respect, and Elizabeth could not help but think his handsomeness remarkable.

"It must worry you to be away from her."

"Her companion is a very trustworthy lady, but I confess I am more at ease when I can be with her."

"It is a remarkably fine morning," she had said, concerned he might think her prying into his personal matters. "I think I might pull back the curtains for Jane when I return to her. I believe a little sunshine might do a world of good for her."

"You are very devoted to your sister."

"She is the dearest creature in the world to me. My mother once said of us when we were younger that if Jane was going to have her head cut off, I would insist that mine be cut off too."

Darcy laughed aloud at this, which had made Elizabeth turn and look at him in surprise. She found that his entire expression changed when he laughed, and it surprised her how much pleasure she took from his reaction. In an attempt to keep her wits about her, Elizabeth reminded herself of his coldness the day before. That person was so different from the man that walked beside her his morning. No, he could not possibly look on her in the same way she did him.

Though Darcy gazed out his bedroom window, his eyes did not see the view it afforded, for his mind was deep in thought. He had known it would be difficult to walk out with Miss Bennet. Her behaviour, her sweetness, everything would serve to undermine even the most steadfast of resolutions. He had noted a blush graced her features when she saw him approach her that morning, but he could not allow it to give him pleasure. That she might come to enjoy him as similarly as he enjoyed being near her would only serve to expose him as indefensibly cruel, for he could never act on any

63

feelings that might arise between them. To hurt such a kind and honourable young lady was inexcusable. She did not deserve to be treated so carelessly.

He remembered the small hand that had rested on his arm, and how it had drawn his eyes up its length to behold her sweet face... how her dark lashes grazed her cheek, her complexion brightened by the exercise. He thought then of her almond-shaped eyes and how they sparkled when she was merry...how they shone when she spoke with conviction...how they lifted as a true smile reached her eyes while she looked upon him. It had become a torture to watch her, to be so near her, and to know that for all of his appreciation of this woman, a love between them could never result in anything but bitter regret. Upon returning from their walk, he had escorted her to the breakfast room and abandoned her there with the intention of answering some missives on matters of business. He had hoped, rather than believed, that it would serve to remind him of his obligations and put his frivolous attraction into perspective.

Chapter Nine

Turning over in the bed, Darcy sighed deeply as he took up his pocket watch. It was after three in the morning, and he could not get to sleep. The information that Elizabeth Bennet had been, and still was, in Town disturbed his false sense of security. There was no getting over her—no, of course not.

How would he face her after what he had done? The guilt of his actions weighed heavily upon him. How could he have allowed himself to behave so unguardedly? It was inexcusable, and the fact that he had come to feel a decided regard for her only served to complicate matters further. A lesser man would have been capable of forgetting her. However, as it was, he instead tortured himself constantly with a pair of fine eyes, saddened with disappointment and pain.

He could not recall the last time he had felt hunger. Every spare instant was seized and consumed by thoughts of Elizabeth. Darcy thought he saw her everywhere. It took little more than the brown, curly locks of a lady's hair to make his heart soar with anticipation, only to plummet moments after, once it became obvious that the woman was someone else. His chest ached at the loss of her, and yet he had no choice but to let her go. Finding himself again wavering over Miss Elizabeth, he took up the worn pages of a letter his uncle had written to him weeks previously.

Tuesday, 31 December, 1811

Fitzwilliam,

Words cannot express the weariness with which I write to you. As I am sure you are aware, my son and heir, Gregory, has chosen to marry a woman of no fortune, no family, no respectability, and is wholly unknown to the world. I need not repeat to you what is being said there in Town, for you have surely experienced it first hand.

My younger son, Edward, has confirmed his intention to speak with you personally over how we must proceed. My wife has taken

66

to her bed, and it grieves me to see her so distressed. Nevertheless, we must not appear to, in any way, shun Gregory, in spite of how dearly he deserves it—but we must not sanction his behaviour either. Though I am sure you are quite informed upon the subject, I fear it is necessary for me to again stress the demands of duty and propriety, for the sake of our family, as it apparently was not made clearly enough to my own children.

By birth, each member of the Fitzwilliam-Darcy-De Bourgh family was given the honour and responsibility associated with our good names. We are meant to serve as a presiding example to the rest of the world by the choices we make, and the actions we take. As a man of this family, you are responsible for the continuation of that standard of respectability and the furthering of connections. The wife you choose and the children she bears will also carry this responsibility to the generations to come.

It goes without saying, that Gregory is thoroughly aware of this same responsibility and even more, as he not only stands to become the next Earl of Desham, but also the head of this family when I am dead. That he has not fulfilled it, only means that the rest of us must work that much harder to compensate for his failing. Not even the smallest gesture of improper behaviour may be tolerated. Every eye in society will be looking to the rest of us to confirm our inadequacy as a great family. We must not, nay, <u>will not</u> give *them more reason to speak badly of us. The entire family's respectability has been called into question, and you and your cousins are now called upon to answer with the utmost comportment.*

Of course, there has not been an instant in my mind that I thought you unaware of these facts, yet there was never an occasion for me to believe I ought to feel concern for Gregory's behaviour. Therefore, I feel I must again express the duty and expectations for my family's good name. I know I will be secure in my trust that you will not fail on this or any account. At any rate, we must be very careful with whom we associate and train our every move to speak of our respectability. You will know how best to communicate this for yourself.

With that point made, I would like you to know that you have grown into a very good man, Fitzwilliam, and your father would have been quite proud of you. I am convinced that we may safely rely on you to make a more prudent match in marriage.

Your aunt sends you her love and begs that you add her to your thoughts as she suffers most cruelly.

Until we meet again—

T. Fitzwilliam

How it pained Darcy to think of his uncle's confidence

in his abilities! He had already failed this command with his actions toward Miss Elizabeth, and again as he now allowed himself to fully acknowledge the extent of his attachment to her. Despite prudence and expectations, he had genuinely fallen in love with her. He had never before considered himself the type of man capable of toying with a lady's feelings. He had always attempted to behave honourably, and yet with Miss Elizabeth, he had somehow lost control of himself. It was without question that he suffered as much, if not more, than the lady herself.

In Elizabeth Bennet, he had found his equal in every particular but consequence. Her intelligence was unquestionable, her heart, genuine. Her personality, so different and yet so similar to his own. He thought her the perfect compliment to himself, as she instinctively knew how to beckon him from his awkward reticence. She was everything that was lovely, and he ached for her. The warmth of her eyes, the comfort of her friendship—he even missed the scent of lavender that floated in the air as she moved. The taste of her lips, so forbidden, had been exquisite, and yet not enough. He could never get enough of the flavour of honeysuckle sweetness he had found in her kiss.

His heart tore in his chest. How badly he wished that he could honour the promise made to her with that kiss! To spend every day of his life with her, basking in the love and happiness he had felt for only a few precious moments. Elizabeth was joy, and he was bereft without her. And still, the barrier between them, once only inconvenient, had been rendered insurmountable by his cousin's scandalous marriage. To marry a woman so beneath him in consequence would only add to his family's grief and further lower them in the world's esteem. Yet, what pained him most was that it was no fault of Miss Bennet's. She could not control her connections or their behaviour.

He had been the one responsible for their attachment. He could have taken measures to ensure she never entertained hopes for their future, and yet he had not been capable of controlling his actions. Each smile, laugh, and happy moment with Elizabeth had only added to his hunger for more. A lifetime would not have been enough of the joy he had felt with Elizabeth.

Indeed, the thought of how his behaviour had injured her only served to make him feel ill. The misery he felt was, in his opinion, only right for what he had done. He had known her to be in love, and he had allowed it to happen. As desperately as he had wished to believe that it was only his feelings that would be wounded at his departure, deep inside, he had known with all his heart that Elizabeth would suffer from his abandonment. Only the constant reading of his uncle's letter reminded him of his responsibility. The raised brows of the *ton* at his expense alone would have meant nothing to him. For his own sake, propriety could be damned!

Yet, it was not only himself he could think of. His sister, his cousins, his aunts and uncle would all feel the effects of his choices. He held a responsibility buried in love for them that prevented him from acting differently. The family could not stand another imprudent action, not now. It was for their sakes he held firm to his wretched, god-forsaken honour. He detested it with all his being, but he could not give way. In any case, he resigned himself likely never to feel whole again. The self-loathing of being his own keeper, yet forced to practice monumental willpower, ate away at him. He did not care to eat, much less be civil in company, and even his dear sister was taking care to avoid him.

He was a slave to his own "good-fortune" in birth and consequence, and he made it quite clear how thoroughly he detested it. He had been born knowing that anything he wished for, he could have—the world was at his fingertips. However, at the age of eight and twenty, he had found the one thing he wanted and could not have. It was a cruel irony that the greater his fortune, the more inaccessible his dear Elizabeth became. She was there, within arm's reach, and yet he could never allow himself to pick that apple from the tree. It was at this moment that he discovered this alleged Garden of Eden was no paradise, not even close—he was living in the midst of Hell itself.

Chapter Ten

Elizabeth dipped her pen in the black ink bottle and attempted to concentrate. She had been seated there for nearly a quarter-hour trying to think of what she might write to her sister, Mary, in Kent. After the last two sleepless nights, her head ached and her tattered sensibilities gave her no relief. Only two days earlier, Bingley had informed them that Mr Darcy would be joining them at Bingley's dinner for Jane. She did not know how she could face him, as she was sure no meeting between them would be comfortable. She suspected that Mr Darcy would take the opportunity to make it very clear that he had no intention of furthering a connection between them.

Elizabeth's stomach lurched at the thought of enduring cold civility from him. *Oh, why did I let this happen to me?* she thought sadly. She knew that she only needed to tell

Jane she preferred to stay home, and her sister would understand. Yet, the masochist that was her heart longed to see him again, no matter the circumstances. Her more reasonable side hoped that his pointed dismissal of her might result in ceasing her love for him. Deep down, she knew that the only result would be to make her feel wretched.

"Lizzy?"

Elizabeth turned at the sounds of her sister's voice. "Mmm?"

"My aunt wondered if you would like to go out with us to the dressmaker's this morning."

She almost declined, but thought better of it, and agreed to go along. It would do her more good, she reasoned, than sitting indoors and mulling over what was inevitable. The fresh air and distraction would certainly improve her spirits. Elizabeth hoped, rather than believed, it would take her mind off matters that were entirely beyond her control.

It almost did not seem real that Jane was to be married. Elizabeth felt as though it was a fact said more than it was meant. However, she knew it was true, and though it meant that Jane would be leaving her, Elizabeth was genuinely happy for her. Mr Bingley was perfect for Jane, good-hearted and genuine, and she knew they would be very content together, though Jane's sisters would miss her terribly.

So it was that Mrs Gardiner and the Misses Bennet set out to visit the dressmaker. It was a very mild afternoon for January—cold, but not unbearable. Nevertheless, Elizabeth was grateful for the hot bricks at her feet as the carriage rode along.

As the Bennets were rarely in Town, Jane and Elizabeth relied on their aunt to know the best places for forming a trousseau. Mrs Gardiner took them to several dress and trinket shops, allowing the girls to buy whatever they liked and Jane to be fitted for her new things. After several hours of admiring various colours of silks and muslins against Jane's lovely complexion, the ladies declared the day a success, and went out to wait for the carriage.

Elizabeth was cheerfully exhausted by the trip, and smiled widely as her bright eyes watched the people passing. Hence, she was not at all prepared for the sight

75

she saw coming toward her at that moment. So distracted was she that she dropped the ribbons of Jane's bonnet, having forgotten her task of tying it completely. Later, she would realize that the moment a person is most likely to appear is when you stop thinking of them.

Darcy paced his study, his humour positively boorish. Another night without sleep, spent regretting the past, had only served to amplify his beastly temper. It was the fourth morning in a row he had left Georgiana to breakfast alone.

He had come to the conclusion in the early hours of the morning that he needed to speak with Miss Bennet. He was honour-bound to give her an explanation for his behaviour. If he could give her nothing else, she at least deserved to know the truth.

Darcy knew that there would never be a good time to give a person such bleak and painful information, and he dreaded the interaction like a soul does death. Despite all his wishes and wants, he could never be what they both needed. Elizabeth deserved, however, an explanation. If it made her hate him or ruined her opinion of him forever, he believed it was only fair. He would rather be loathed than loved by her in this situation, as it meant she would be liberated of him. Darcy could not bear to think of her forever unhappy at his hand. He hoped for anything but that. She ought not suffer for him—she was the innocent in this, and he the rogue. He knew it was his duty to do whatever he could to set her free.

"Brother?" Georgiana's sweet voice rang timidly in the air and served to return his thoughts to the present. He looked at her in surprise. It was unusual to see her in his study. Out of respect or fear, he knew not which, Darcy's little sister never ventured to disturb him here. It had been some time since she had attempted thusly—not since *before*.

"Ana," he said, forcing himself to smile warmly. It was not entirely difficult as his sister was very dear to him. She hurried forward to receive a hug. "You are unhappy with me," he predicted.

"No, never. Only I—have I displeased you, Fitzwilliam?"

"Of course not, my dearest," he sighed. His thoughtless brooding and skipping meals had evidently worried his sister. He should have known better.

"I did not think as much," Georgiana continued, and Darcy ascertained that she was clearly attempting to muster enough bravery to question him. "You are troubled, Brother, and I would be remiss if I did not notice it. Will you not confide in me?"

Darcy looked into her hopeful, bright eyes, dark brown like his own. She was the very image of his mother and became more like her every day. He led her to sit with him, and he kissed her small fingers. Pensively, he held her hand in his and studied it while he decided how to answer. She was not a child, not anymore, and was quickly growing into a young woman right before his eyes. Yet, his propensity to shield her from everything was instinctive—it was difficult to think of her as a confidant, though he knew she would be superior to any he could find elsewhere.

"You are right, my mind has been over-occupied of late. Some of it I am not at liberty to speak of, though I have also been very distracted with this business of Gregory's marriage. He has placed us all in a very uncomfortable position, and has required much of my attention of late. The other, thankfully, is not at all grave. Charles Bingley has informed me he is to be married."

Georgiana's face broke into a large smile. "Oh Fitzwilliam! That is wonderful news! He must be so happy!"

Darcy smiled. "Yes, I believe he is."

"Are you to stand up with him? What is the lady's name? When is the wedding?"

Darcy chuckled at his sister's enthusiasm. "Yes, I have agreed to stand up with him, and he is to be married to a Miss Jane Bennet of Hertfordshire. The wedding is to be in February."

"Bennet? The same family you wrote of? Your friends?"

"Yes, though they were certainly more the friends of Bingley than myself."

"So this is the lady he favoured."

"The very one."

Georgiana smiled at the thought. "What a lovely story they will have to tell their children."

Darcy's smile faltered a bit, but he kept his composure. "Indeed."

"Brother, are you worried for Mr Bingley?"

"No, I am very happy for him."

"Then what keeps you so troubled as to prevent you from staying in my company? It is not only at breakfast I have missed you. You remained closed up in here for most of yesterday. You cannot be so concerned for my cousin as this. It has been weeks since we learned of his marriage."

Darcy smiled sadly. "I am afraid, dear one, the rest is what I am not at liberty to speak of."

Georgiana gripped his hand tightly. "I understand. But it pains me to see you so unhappy."

Darcy lowered his head and nodded. "Perhaps a day out might improve our spirits. What do you say?"

Georgiana agreed eagerly, her expression changing to excitement. "Might we go shopping? I would like to purchase a gift for Mrs Annesley."

Darcy shook his head—his sister's companion had admittedly been all but forgotten in the past two months. "Ah, yes, it is her birthday this week, is it not? I am relieved you have remembered."

"May we go?"

Darcy nodded in the affirmative, and Georgiana hurriedly went upstairs to ready herself. He watched her go, thankful for the diversion this excursion would afford. They had not visited three shops before Georgiana found the perfect gift for her companion. While Mrs Annesley did not care for bright ornaments, Georgiana was certain the lady would like a pair of tortoise-shell combs similar to a pair of her own that Mrs. Annesley had often admired.

Pleased with their purchase, the siblings left the shop and were preparing to cross the street to look at ribbons when Darcy stopped in his tracks, eyes wide with shock. They must have seen one another at the same moment, as Miss Elizabeth froze at the sight of him.

"Come," he said, recollecting himself and taking the hand of his thoroughly confused sister.

Jane Bennet was the first to acknowledge them, and she curtseyed with a smile. "Mr Darcy."

"Miss Bennet, Miss Elizabeth," he said in reciprocation. "Allow me to introduce my sister, Georgiana."

Georgiana blushed, but managed to greet them shyly.

"Aunt, allow me to introduce you to Mr Darcy," Jane continued. "Mr Darcy, this is my aunt, Mrs Edward Gardiner."

"I am very pleased to meet you, madam," he said, inspecting the lady carefully.

"Thank you, sir."

Darcy watched Elizabeth as Georgiana was addressed by Miss Bennet and Mrs Gardiner. He noticed easily that her colour was high, and he felt for her discomfort, so similar to his own.

"I hope you are well, Miss Elizabeth."

"I am, thank you," she said, looking anywhere but at him.

"And your family? Are they well?"

"They are, thank you for enquiring."

Darcy chose then to be merciful and avoid questioning her further. "I believe congratulations are in order, Miss Bennet. I am very happy for you and Mr Bingley."

The polite conversation continued until the two parties found an excuse to part ways. The interaction had been very uncomfortable to say the least. Darcy unhappily took note of Elizabeth's sad expression and tired features. She was as lovely as he remembered, but he could determine a change in her. There was but one smile, offered at the introduction of Georgiana, and the rest of her demeanour was consumed with nervousness that had replaced her customary ease. He miserably knew it was because of him, and spent the carriage ride home silently staring out the window.

"That was, I suppose, the trouble you were not at liberty to speak of," Georgiana said gently as she removed her gloves in the hallway. He looked at her in surprise, but she had not waited for a response. Wretchedly, he watched her disappear up the stairs before returning to his study, closing the door with a resounding thud behind him.

Chapter Eleven

"Do not ask me questions," Elizabeth said firmly as Jane sat on their bed that night.

"Why must you keep secrets?" Jane pleaded.

"You know as well as I that some stories are better left untold."

Jane worriedly watched her sister comb her dark, curly hair in the mirror. Elizabeth had gone straight to her room upon their return that afternoon. When she had come down for supper, Jane had noted that her sister had been crying. She dearly wished Elizabeth would confide in her.

"It was quite a surprise to see Mr Darcy this morning. His sister seemed very kind—and lovely."

"Miss Darcy was very beautiful," Elizabeth agreed. "She and her brother favour one another considerably.

84

"Yes." Jane took the hairbrush from her sister's hand and began brushing Elizabeth's hair herself. "Lizzy, we both know you are not obligated to tell me, and I know you well enough to understand that you certainly shall not if you are not inclined, but I beg you not to suffer silently. I know it must be very hard to see Mr Darcy again."

Elizabeth shifted uncomfortably. "I believe I made my sentiments on that subject known to you in the letter I wrote before you came to Town. Mr Darcy and I are common acquaintances, that is all."

Jane pursed her lips, but she did not argue. She did silently note that one was not often induced to tears by a common acquaintance. She laid down the brush and began braiding Elizabeth's hair. It was very hard for her not to push her younger sister to speak of her feelings, but she reminded herself there was virtue in not asking questions for which she required no answer.

"Mr Darcy has agreed to stand up with Charles at my wedding. I was very glad. I knew how badly Charles wanted his friend to be there."

Elizabeth did not venture a reply, and Jane chewed her lip, pressed for some sort of conversation. At last, she was resigned to silence and tied her sister's braid with a ribbon. Elizabeth caught Jane's hand before she could pull it away.

"How shall I do without you?"

Jane smiled. "We will write, and you will come to visit me often. Charles thinks very highly of you, and I cannot see him unhappy to have you stay with us."

Elizabeth smiled, but Jane saw it did not reach her eyes.

"Lizzy—"

"Trust me, Jane?"

Jane sighed and nodded. Despite wanting an explanation badly, she knew that the kindest thing would be to support her sister now. By the time she finished tying back her own hair, Elizabeth was in bed, eyes closed. Resolutely, Jane blew out the candle and climbed in beside her. She sent up a silent prayer that all would be well.

*

Elizabeth waited until she was sure Jane was sleeping before creeping out of the room and downstairs. Candle in hand, she curled up in the windowsill and rested her chin on her knees. Seeing Mr Darcy that day had done nothing to cure her frustration of feelings. His looks, his conversation, everything about the interaction had spoke of mere acquaintanceship. She did not know how else he could have behaved without being inappropriate, but it had stung nonetheless. It was there her uncle found her in the morning, curled up in the windowsill asleep, her candle long burnt out, and she nowhere closer to finding her peace of mind.

Chapter Twelve

The evening of Bingley's dinner party soon arrived, deriving equal parts anxiety and anticipation from the attendants. Although she would have firmly denied it, Elizabeth had taken a great deal of time on her appearance. She wore a gown of mint green silk with matching ribbons woven in her hair. She was exceptionally lovely and more nervous than she had ever felt. Elizabeth had visited the Bingley townhouse many times in the daytime with her sister, but the night seemed to grant it a mysterious air. Her aunt's hand coming to rest on her back reminded Elizabeth to keep moving. She was not surprised to learn that Mr and Miss Darcy were already arrived.

Despite her rapidly beating heart and inner turmoil, the evening had gone rather well. Even so, the comfortable friendship Elizabeth and Mr Darcy had once enjoyed in Hertfordshire had vanished. They could scarcely look at one another. Mr Darcy had retreated behind some sort of expressionless mask, and it was impossible for Elizabeth to read him. In truth, while this pained her, Elizabeth was relieved that Mr Darcy had not gone out of his way to ignore her pointedly as some young men were wont to do. She told herself that this was right. Their friendship had taken them so far outside the dictates of propriety that they were now obligated to return to the beginning. Despite that, though, Elizabeth knew herself to be blushing every minute of the evening. How dearly she envied Darcy's mask! As a woman, she found it more difficult to conceal every emotion she felt. The more valiantly she attempted to disguise her discomfort, the brighter her blush became, imagining that every creature in the room was aware of her silliness.

After eating, Miss Darcy was convinced to entertain them on the pianoforte—saying that she would play for them if they would not make her sing.

With her brother so caught up in Miss Bennet, Miss Bingley found herself required to hold conversation with the Gardiners, as Mr Darcy had gone over to turn pages for his sister. Grateful to be ignored, Elizabeth kept her expression as neutral as possible while her uncle and aunt skilfully endured the patronizing conversation of their hostess. One of many glances at Darcy confirmed that he had a similar plan by removing himself to the pianoforte. Throughout supper, he had seemed scarcely interested in anything and had contributed almost nothing to any topic discussed. In any case, Elizabeth knew him to dislike speaking amongst a group, preferring only to speak when there was but one other. Having had many such interactions, Elizabeth knew that he did, in fact, have a great deal of intelligent conversation when he wished it. He turned to look at her then, their eyes locking. She was unprepared, unsure of what message she wanted to send with her gaze. She searched his eyes for the slightest bit of understanding. All she could find was overwhelming sadness. Its effect was so powerful, Elizabeth broke away and stared at her lap until she could regain her composure. The expression of his eyes she locked away inside her memory to decipher later.

For that moment, she concentrated on everything but him. Briefly, she discerned that Miss Bingley was giving Mrs Gardiner her opinions on lace. Elizabeth listened attentively until the turmoil of her thoughts was interrupted by the discussion of fabric. By the time Miss Bingley had moved to muslin, Elizabeth had regained her bearings. She opted not to look at Darcy again.

فلبه

"Have you now seen what I have been saying all along is true?" Elizabeth asked when the candles were out.

"I could not comprehend what I saw tonight," Jane said, lying beside her in the bed.

"Any connection that ever existed in my mind or in anyone else's is impossible. It no longer exists because he clearly wishes to communicate that he is not interested in furthering *any* sort of acquaintance between us."

Elizabeth watched Jane frown and shift uncomfortably in the moonlight.

"I cannot understand it."

"It is not so complicated, Jane. Mr Darcy's attentions to me are over. We are meant to move on with our lives." She struggled to give her sweet sister a confident look, and changed the subject. "Did you enjoy your party, Jane? It *was* for you."

Jane smiled sweetly. "I did. Charles makes me so happy, Lizzy! Tonight I felt as though we were already married with our dear family around us."

"I am glad to hear it. Mr Bingley could scarcely keep his eyes off of you all evening. I do believe that with you in the room, everyone else ceases to exist for him."

"Do you think he was negligent to his other guests?"

"No," Elizabeth laughed. "Just beside himself with love for you."

Jane blushed prettily. "Sometimes I do not think I deserve so much happiness."

"But you do, dear Jane. Your goodness has been rewarded, and you must not feel guilt for your happiness, only gratitude—and you must miss *me* very much when you are gone."

"I will miss you very much, as you well know," Jane laughed, "but perhaps not so very much if you are willing to go along with our plan."

"Plan?"

"Charles mentioned tonight that it might be a good thing for you to come and stay with us for a while once we are settled." When Elizabeth did not immediately respond, Jane continued. "He thought it might be nice to have you there with me—as I will have almost no acquaintances in Yorkshire."

Elizabeth was silent for several moments. It seemed as though she was to be away more than she was home this year. Her mind was a jumble, unable to determine what it was she wanted to do. "May I think on it and give you my answer later?"

"Of course," Jane replied, rolling over to sleep. "Goodnight, Lizzy."

Elizabeth lay awake for very long while that night—she could not remember the last time she had gone to sleep easily. Her thoughts swirled in her mind without order, and her heart felt ragged and bruised. She had spent an entire evening in Darcy's company and survived. For all appearances, she had accepted that what was done, was done, and she felt that it was all she could do for now.

Yet, the sadness in his eyes had worried her. It had spoken volumes, and still she could not make it out completely. The one point she had determined, however, was that there was no hope left. Those sad brown eyes had held all the hopeless regret that she felt inside. It had been difficult to see, but it had given her the confirmation she so badly needed. It had not been a dream. Two months earlier they had fallen in love, against all odds, and they had kissed outside at the Netherfield Ball. Time and removal had begun to combine and make her question that truth. But his eyes—his eyes that night had confirmed what she knew. They had loved. It was no dream....

Chapter Thirteen

Georgiana's gentle hand on his forearm brought Darcy back to the present. She had been singing softly at the pianoforte, her skill lulling him away from the present. He saw her then, as she sat beside him, offering her support in her own quiet way. Darcy smiled briefly, but neither of them said more. They had always known how to communicate without speaking. In silence, he accepted her comfort, and they remained that way for some time.

Seeing Elizabeth that evening had done little to decrease his resolution to speak to her. So little did he like the thought, and yet it was all he could think of. Her eyes, like windows to her emotions, had shown him the depth of her confusion and hurt at being abandoned by him. Not for the first time, Darcy wished he had never gone to Hertfordshire with Bingley.

"Brother?"

"Mmm?"

"I am going to bed. You should as well."

"Goodnight," he said as she kissed his cheek. He knew he ought to go as she said, but he was not quite ready to face the darkness that would come soon enough as it was.

He knew that the sooner he spoke to Elizabeth, the better and the more quickly she would recover, and yet he disliked the finality of the gesture. The conversation would end all that was unsaid between them. He dreaded causing her pain. He swiftly penned a note to Bingley, and then sent himself to bed. Let his friend unknowingly decide the date. It was far better than determining it himself.

Darcy's note had suggested he go along for Bingley's next intended trip to the Gardiner residence, though Bingley was sure he had no idea why Darcy would wish to accompany him on the visit. Bingley had read the note over three times and determined that he would answer by calling at the Darcy townhouse that afternoon. He was ushered into the library where he located Darcy studying a large tome very carefully.

"Bingley! To what have I the honour of this visit?" Darcy queried, looking up with surprise.

Bingley seated himself without invitation. "I received your message. Darcy, I confess I find it puzzled me exceedingly."

"Oh?"

"Yes. You see, I cannot understand your motive for wishing to visit the Misses Bennet." Darcy did not answer immediately, and Bingley watched his friend closely. "Darcy, have you not done enough in that corner?"

Darcy appeared momentarily alarmed, but quickly overcame it. "I have done little to recommend myself to them, I know."

"Then I must ask what the reason is that you feel you must provoke them. If there had been any doubt that you no longer cared for Miss Elizabeth, you did what you could last evening to make it a certainty."

In his infuriating way, Darcy did not react in demeanour or with words, preferring only to twist his signet ring pensively.

"Bingley, I will not attempt to explain myself to you, for there is nothing I wish to make known to anyone. However, I assure you that this visit shall be my very last."

Bingley left his chair in frustration. He was agitated and unsure if he ought to allow it. He suspected that Jane would not appreciate Darcy speaking to her sister again.

"Darcy, you are the dearest friend in the world to me, and I would do almost anything to repay you for all that you have given me. However, Miss Elizabeth will be my sister in two weeks' time, and it will be my duty to protect her—even from you."

"In a fortnight, I assure you there will be no need to protect her from me."

Bingley noted an edge of impatience in Darcy's voice. Knowing his friend was becoming irritated, Bingley chose to take his time before responding again.

"Charles," Darcy said quietly, "I am aware that what I am asking requires you to go against your nature, and your every instinct commands you to reject it. But I ask you as my friend to allow me one more interview with her. I give you my word that this is indeed the only time I will ask something like this of you."

Bingley sighed and turned to look into the fire burning in the hearth. Darcy was a difficult man to refuse. This was compounded by the fact that Darcy had been the closest friend and mentor that he had ever had in his life. It gave Bingley pause. He knew well enough that Darcy would never ask for something of this nature if he did not think it absolutely necessary. Reluctantly, Bingley relented.

"I visit Miss Bennet tomorrow at three in the afternoon. If you are climbing into my carriage at the precise moment I mean to leave, I will not prevent you from accompanying me."

Darcy nodded once and said nothing.

"I will leave you now," Bingley said, walking to the door. Before he exited, he added, "And Darcy?"

His friend raised his face at the sound of his name.

"Do not make me regret this decision."

Chapter Fourteen

Elizabeth was reading to one of the children when Mr Bingley was announced with Mr Darcy. She looked wide-eyed at her sister in shock. Jane's similarly surprised expression was enough to convince Elizabeth that she had not been a party to any scheme.

"I hope you do not mind," Bingley said in his usually cheerful way. "Darcy expressed a wish to join me on my visit with you all this afternoon."

"Not at all," said Jane, who found her voice first. "You are very welcome, Mr Darcy."

In her great confusion, Elizabeth kept her eyes lowered and said nothing. She had not been at all prepared for Mr Darcy to come that afternoon. A sense of foreboding settled in her stomach.

Bingley and Darcy exchanged a look. Bingley spoke again, "I thought we might go for a walk if that is agreeable?"

The ladies acquiesced, and they all started off toward a nearby park. Soon Jane and Bingley reluctantly trailed away from Mr Darcy and Elizabeth. When Darcy turned to step into a small copse of trees, Elizabeth instinctively followed him. She walked to a bench and seated herself. He had said almost nothing on the walk over, and Elizabeth could sense that whatever the reason he had for cornering her in this way, it was not to be a happy occasion. She steeled herself for his speech, her heart already feeling painfully swollen inside her chest. He paced in front of her, turned his back, then around again to look her in the eyes. Elizabeth swallowed audibly, the gulp resounding in both of their ears.

"I have treated you abominably. I cannot reflect upon it without pain," he said softly. "Whatever you think of me, I absolutely deserve. I can never make amends for how I have acted, so I will not trouble you for forgiveness. I have no excuse for myself, yet despite my

101

most fervent determination to control my feelings, I fell in love against my will, in spite of every attempt to prevent it. You captivated me, took hold in my heart and I was helpless. You are unlike any woman I have ever known, and you somehow surpass them in every thing—there is no comparison to you, Miss Bennet."

The glaze of unshed tears in his eyes invited Elizabeth's own emotions to take control. She tried desperately not to cry, but she had determined that this was no proposal. Whatever it could be called, this was certainly its opposite—he was letting her go. How little prepared she was for this painful admission! She tried fervently to control her breathing.

"I am ashamed of myself, Miss Bennet. No matter my feelings, I should never have imposed myself upon you as I did at the Netherfield Ball. It was inexcusable. I know not what came over me—I should not have departed before expressing my sincerest apologies. You did not deserve such misbehaviour. I cannot tell you—"

"Mr Darcy, sir, I beg you, speak plainly. We are beyond such formality. Say what you must—but say it without such reserve, if you please. You owe me this."

At this, his shoulders seemed to droop, and Elizabeth straightened her spine with a deep breath. To her surprise, he came to sit beside her on the bench. He studied he ground for quite some time before speaking again.

"Elizabeth, my cousin, the heir to the Desham Earldom, has disgraced my family with a marriage of the most imprudent kind. If he had been intending it, he could not have located a more unsuitable young woman. She is with literally no family or connections. No one has any accounting of her coming to be. She is a foundling, and most likely a gentleman's natural child. It has left us all in uproar. It falls now to my cousins and me to repair what can be mended of the family's reputation. It is for this reason I cannot offer you marriage. A connection that might have once been begrudgingly overlooked will now only fuel the destruction wrought by gossip and further lower my ancestors' good name to an irreparable level. I must also think of my sister's prospects in wake of this unfortunate occurrence. You are not at fault. It is I who must place this wretched situation firmly on my own

103

shoulders. I have brought us here; it is I who should feel it."

Elizabeth rose from the bench and turned her back to him. Her voice was a sob when she spoke. "You are forgetting something, Mr Darcy. You must remember that you were not the only one of us to fall in love. I craved your attentions, I encouraged them, I wanted you to kiss me! It is not only your own heart that ignored its owner's wishes. I knew you could never marry me, and yet I was helpless in what took place. It was wrong of us, but it could not have been helped."

Darcy frowned silently at the ground in front of him. Elizabeth turned to face him, and he lifted his eyes to reveal the tears that had finally spilled onto his cheeks.

"I am so sorry, Elizabeth."

She closed her eyes from the sight, her body trembling with repressed sobs. "In another time, another place, we might have been very happy together."

She came to sit back down on the bench beside him. Looking around to assure himself they were alone, he placed his palm on her cheek and kissed her gently— she tasted the salt of their mingled tears.

"I love you, Fitzwilliam," she whispered. "I-I thought you ought to hear it, just this one time."

Darcy pulled out his handkerchief and dried her tears, she leaned into his touch. "Lizzy, why do you not despise me?" he said softly, searching her eyes.

"How can I? I cannot when I know you are suffering as much as I."

He nodded, but he said no more. There was nothing left to say.

She watched him examine the handkerchief in his hands, still wet with her tears. "I think I should prefer to return back on my own. Thank you for telling me, Mr Darcy. You are a good man."

"I have never felt less so," he admitted quietly.

ﻋﻠﮯ

Upon returning to her uncle's, Elizabeth could not excuse herself quickly enough. After her conversation with Mr Darcy, she had felt the painful emotions that constricted her chest threatening to spill over with every step she took. She collapsed upon her bed, bitter tears falling hotly onto the pillow she held tightly to her lips, stifling her sobs. Never in her life had she felt so miserable, so helpless. Darcy had become her ideal, then turned into the only man that consumed her heart, demanding response from her very soul. She loved him with a power she had never experienced, and yet she had known all along that such girlish hopes were in vain.

Mr Darcy was a very rich and grand gentleman. Society watched his every move eagerly, his time was his own, but his wishes could not rule his life. He had said he loved her, begged her to understand his struggle, and they had cried together. There was no way for him to escape his duty, no way for him to marry her. Elizabeth felt her body shake involuntarily with the force of her sobs.

He did not understand that she asked for so little. If she could but have his love forever, she would have been content. It was at this time in her life that Elizabeth understood what drove some women to live improperly with a man. She knew she would never resort to that, and Darcy would never ask that of her, knowing she loved him. She would spend her life a maiden—no

106

home of her own, no children, or husband to love—alone. How could she ever act as a respectable wife when her heart was irrevocably captured by another? If she could not have Mr Darcy, then she would have no man. She was not the type of woman to transfer her affections. No, they were to be fixed forever on one man.

Elizabeth wondered if she might ever have the strength to leave the bed where she lay, the room she was in, cease the tears that she cried. Such calm behaviour seemed beyond her. How could she leave and pretend that her heart was not shattered? Would she ever smile or even laugh again? She did not think it possible. Darcy would marry another woman with a large dowry, a darling of the *ton*, and incomparably handsome. He would forget her and his declarations. Worse yet, he would live to regret disclosing such feelings for her and the time in his life where their paths had crossed. She, however, would never forget him. His name was branded on her heart, and she would take her love for him to the grave. Elizabeth could never dishonour her feelings by marrying another. She would not stain them with caprice. Her heart would never be touched again. It belonged to one man, whether he chose to claim it not.

Elizabeth could not fault his decision, though she hated the circumstances that brought it about. She dared not imagine what might have been if things had been different. A knock at the door disturbed her misery. She gulped for air and endeavoured to silence her whimpering.

"Lizzy?" a small voice she recognized to be Jane's asked from the other side of the door.

"Yes?" she said, her voice hoarse.

"Please let me in. I know you are upset."

"I cannot, Jane, please leave me be."

"Lizzy, I cannot be easy knowing you are so distressed."

Elizabeth did not answer. She closed her eyes and breathed rhythmically until she felt her sister give way and return downstairs. What could Jane comprehend of this in her happy state? Every day she was assured of Mr Bingley's love for her. He had promised Jane that they would be together all the days of their lives. She could not know of the aching emptiness that Elizabeth felt or the cruelty of knowing her dearest wish could never be. She could not bear to see Jane now.

It was a full two days before Elizabeth chose to leave her bedroom at the Gardiners'. Despite poor Jane's begging, she had not been capable of convincing her younger sister to eat or come downstairs for a few hours. The family had been coming very close to applying force when Elizabeth appeared as the family was taking breakfast. Without speaking, Elizabeth took a seat beside Jane. They all greeted her in genuine surprise, and Elizabeth flexed her facial muscles in the shape of a smile. A little cajoling from Jane convinced Elizabeth to nibble a slice of dry toast.

Elizabeth felt as though she no longer existed. The only confirmation that she was alive was the constant throbbing of her heart. The rest of her reality felt like the details of a painting—rich, vibrant, perfectly dimensioned; yet nothing was real. The spoon beside her plate, the velvet curtains over the windows, the dirt on the carpet, were all props for the exquisite still life that was her existence—a sadness that would not abate.

She could scarcely countenance the concerned expressions on the faces of her loved ones. How it must have pained them to see their vibrant Lizzy so cast down, and yet, she could not care. When she felt as though her appearance was sufficiently executed, she rose from her seat and abandoned her half-eaten slice of toast to retire upstairs. It was an improvement, she reckoned, for she had left her chambers for a time— something she had despaired of ever doing again.

A deep frown creased Jane's beautiful features as she wrote furiously to her fiancé. She was determined to know what had happened to Elizabeth in the park. She was simply not Elizabeth anymore. Never in her life had Jane felt more helpless. Never had Elizabeth erected a wall so insurmountable. She had been sure her sister would allow her inside to sleep, but Jane was only granted entrance long enough to transfer her belongings elsewhere. Elizabeth did not wish to speak, could not allow for affection, even the presence of others could not be endured above a quarter-hour. Such behaviour was something she and Elizabeth would have laughed at in the past, yet now Elizabeth was drowning, and Jane could not help her. She felt an irrational anger at Bingley for allowing Darcy unsupervised time with Elizabeth. In truth, Jane longed for any outlet that would allow her to give vent to her feelings. She was lost for what to do now. A sudden idea coming to her, Jane dropped her pen and hurried upstairs. Forcefully, she banged on Elizabeth's door.

"Elizabeth, now this is *enough*! I demand you let me in," she said in a tone rarely heard from her. "We are not at home, Lizzy, and we owe our uncle more than this!"

The door opened, and Jane watched her sister turn away and return to the windowsill, where she sat and rested cheek against the glass. Immediately, Jane regretted speaking so harshly to her sister—though it apparently was the only effective method.

"Close the door," Elizabeth said softly when Jane entered the room.

Jane waited there, silently seated before Elizabeth, taking in her swollen eyes and chapped lips. Jane reached up to tuck a curl behind her sister's ear. She had never seen Elizabeth more unkempt or so unhappy. Her sister's eyes had always laughed or danced with mischief. To see her eyes so sad and tilted down at the corners broke Jane's heart.

"He loved me," Elizabeth murmured simply, "but it was not enough."

Jane could not understand the sentiment. She had always considered love—the thing poets waxed romantically to be all-encompassing—was meant to outweigh the pains of the outside world. In her innocent eyes, love was perseverance, and she stated as much to Elizabeth.

"Love may withstand every attempt to dissuade it, I grant you that, but it cannot enable us to be happy if the world does not permit it. To be loved may sometimes be more painful than to be rejected and scorned. I am bereft of feeling, Jane. The only voice in my heart lends itself to what can never be."

"I do not understand."

A sob escaped Elizabeth's lips at this. "Oh, Jane. I hope you never do!"

Chapter Fifteen

It was a torture to remain upright, but Darcy managed it as he attempted valiantly to keep his attention on Bingley, who was pacing in front of him. He had done nothing for three days but sit desolately in his study, staring blankly at the wall in front of him, protectively clutching the handkerchief used to dry Elizabeth's tears. After Darcy had returned from Gracechurch Street, he had gone upstairs and vomited violently, emptying more of his stomach than he believed there had been to give. While he no longer could manage to be sick, the nausea lingered. He felt acidic, achingly empty and his head throbbed painfully. The sadness he had brought to his beloved seemed to gnaw at the very core of him.

"I trusted you, Darcy! I permitted you to see her, to speak with her, and for what purpose? Do you think I would have allowed you to see her if I had known your intentions?"

"I believed it was necessary to conceal my intentions to spare you from making that decision."

A glare from Bingley communicated what he thought of that explanation. "Jane is furious with me. She writes that Miss Elizabeth will not leave her room, and she blames me for allowing whatever occurred between you and her sister."

Darcy's stomach lurched at that information. He clenched the arms of his chair painfully. "Charles, I—"

Bingley put up his hand, and Darcy noted his expression had softened considerably. "I did not come here to quarrel with you. I know you too well to accuse you of duplicity or of treating Miss Elizabeth with cruelty. I supposed I would find you in a similar state today—it is clear I was correct."

"I shall not attempt to make excuses for myself—I deserve no such consideration, I assure you."

Bingley nodded and seated himself. "You are not looking your best, my friend. You are exhausted."

Darcy nodded. "I suppose you have heard of what has taken place with my cousin." He watched as comprehension seeped into Bingley's features. "Everything must now be taken into consideration with this in mind."

"And so you told her the truth."

Darcy said nothing. No confirmation of what had happened would leave his lips. Nevertheless, Bingley did not require such an explicit explanation.

"What a miserable situation!"

"Indeed," Darcy replied.

Bingley appeared to be thinking hard, and both men were silent for some time. Finally, Bingley seemed to have come to a conclusion and spoke. "If you wish to forego attending my wedding, I will understand."

"I leave that for you to decide. You are my dearest friend, and no matter my own personal circumstances, it would still be an honour to stand up with you."

Bingley nodded. "I cannot dispute your goodness, not even in the face of such misfortunes."

"I find I cannot be so kind to myself. Nevertheless, if you wish it, I will be there in a week's time."

"Thank you, Darcy."

"And will you be returning to Hertfordshire soon?"

"Yes, we shall return the day after tomorrow. When may I expect you?"

"I shall only stay one night. I will join you the day before and depart after the wedding breakfast."

Bingley nodded. "Until then, my friend."

Darcy reached out and shook his hand. "Until then."

Elizabeth had never been so relieved to return to Longbourn. Kitty and Lydia's silliness and her mother's animated expressions seemed refreshingly normal. Her father had expressed his relief to see her again, and she had embraced him tightly, inhaling his familiar scent. Indeed, even the smell of Longbourn house was comforting. She was home—where everyone loved her unconditionally, if in their own way.

Mrs Bennet was beside herself dealing with wedding preparations, menus, and place settings for the breakfast after the ceremony. Elizabeth owned that this was her mother's element. If there was anything she did well, her mother was a fine hostess and mistress to Longbourn house. Nary a detail slipped under her nose without detection, and Elizabeth knew that she would only be so lucky to have such domestic skill. Consequently, Jane had left all of her wedding planning to her mother, knowing that she enjoyed it so and would undoubtedly do a superior job in any case.

The first news Elizabeth received upon her return was that her sister Mary and Mr Collins were expecting a child mid-autumn. The family was very glad for her, and Elizabeth wrote a letter expressing her sincerest congratulations.

When the new feeling of being home again began to wane, Elizabeth did everything she could to keep her hands busy and her mind away from London. She did not dare permit herself to consider having to face Mr Darcy one last time for Jane's wedding. She wondered how much more she would have to endure before she was truly permitted to go on. Certainly, he would always be in her life. He was Bingley's dearest friend and would, consequently, be expected to visit often and be a topic of conversation for them all. Elizabeth told

117

herself that if she could only compose herself long enough for Jane's wedding, she could allow herself to slip back into the melancholy she so badly craved. While she was once so disposed to happiness, the feeling now felt very foreign and unnatural to her.

In the face of all this, the wedding of Jane and Bingley was upon them in three days' time. Elizabeth thought Jane looked truly angelic in her white, satin gown. In her sister's hair, Elizabeth had woven pink ribbon gently through her golden locks. Standing amongst her sisters and mother, they all declared Jane breathtakingly beautiful with tears in their eyes.

When the time came, Mr Bennet smiled as he gave Jane into Mr Bingley's care, and Elizabeth found herself again face to face with Mr Darcy. There they were, at an altar, before God and a rector, listening to the sacred words that had been spoken at wedding ceremonies for hundreds of years. Elizabeth noted then that this was perhaps the closest she would ever come to experiencing a wedding for herself—with the man she loved. For a greedy moment, she permitted herself to imagine that this was their wedding, that they were

118

together, that this was *their* happy ending. Too soon, however, the ceremony ended, and Elizabeth was required to return to her own reality.

True to his gentlemanlike character, Darcy kept his distance from her at the wedding breakfast. To be forced to form a neutral conversation with him now would be too cruel and nearly impossible. He stayed only as long as was proper, then departed as quickly as he had come. It was over. He was gone. Elizabeth was unsure what was felt more keenly at that understanding—relief or pain.

She excused herself to walk outside of Longbourn. It was a cruel trick that every place in her life represented a memory of him. Her entire world was now tainted by memories of happier times, of falling in love with a man she still considered to be the best of men. Indeed, she knew she would never again look at her uncle's residence in London with the same eyes. It would forever, in her mind, be associated with Darcy, their conversation in the park, and those painful days that followed. It seemed that wherever she chose to look, she found a place his fingers had touched. They left a mark—even if it was one seen only by her. The thought was overwhelming, something that encompassed her always. His presence in the world would forever be worn on her mind and heart—she would never escape it, she would never try.

"Lizzy?"

Elizabeth turned her head to see her sister. She smiled warmly.

"I could not find you inside and came looking. We shall be leaving soon, and I wanted to say goodbye to you."

Elizabeth hugged her sister. "I am so happy for you! I will miss you dreadfully."

Jane pulled back, but kept hold of her sister's hands. "Have you thought any more of coming to Yorkshire when we are settled?"

Elizabeth paused. Indeed it had been pushed to the back of her mind of late. She studied Jane carefully. "Do you truly wish it? I will not be imposing?"

"No, indeed! It would be a great comfort to have you with me in such a strange place," Jane insisted eagerly.

Elizabeth made a decision then. It would be a place completely new, a place untouched by memories of Mr

Darcy. It was the most sensible decision she felt she had made in months. "If you are positive, Jane, then when you send for me, rest assured, I will come."

Chapter Sixteen

Elizabeth looked out the window as the carriage pulled her closer to Yorkshire. Her brother, Mr Bingley, had sent it for her to travel the four-day excursion, providing the adequate protection due to her as his unmarried sister. She was not afraid to journey alone— quite the contrary. The days travelling the countryside bestowed a much-needed silence for Elizabeth. She *did* look forward to seeing Jane again, and *did* think the change in scenery would be beneficial. She only prayed little would be asked of her in the way of social niceties. Surely Jane and Bingley would wish to venture out in society. She hoped, however, that she would not be expected to accompany them. She had no taste for new friendships and sought only peace and solitude.

The trip was long with frequent stops and temperatures lowering as they ventured further north. Elizabeth was very relieved to be informed of their imminent arrival, and watched with interest as Darnwell's landscape came into view. It was a well-situated seaside estate, and it gave Elizabeth pleasure to imagine her sister living there. Jane and Bingley were waiting outside for her when she arrived, and the sisters embraced dearly at being thus reunited.

"Oh, Lizzy, I am so glad to see you," Jane whispered, holding Elizabeth tight.

"And I you," Elizabeth agreed, pulling back to get a better look at her sister. Jane looked very well indeed. Her cheeks were rosy with happiness, and her eyes twinkled with true joy. Elizabeth was very glad to see it—Jane deserved nothing less. After evading a few questions after her own well-being, Elizabeth was permitted to escape upstairs to rest from her journey. She closed the door to her bedchamber and leaned against it, exhaling lightly. She felt such relief to be far from Longbourn, London, and Mr Darcy—and though her memories followed, the removal from it all seemed to lift a heavy weight from her chest. A moment longer, and she felt she might have suffocated beneath its consequence.

Darcy walked the length of the dance-line, the noise of the ball blurring into a dull roar. It was his first outing since his return to London, and his experience was not boding well for the season. Every woman he met fell into one category: not Elizabeth. A lady's eyes were too large, her chin too prominent, her height too tall, her chest too flat. No woman compared to his Elizabeth, and he was miserable. He looked directly at Colonel Fitzwilliam, the man who had insisted he attend, and crossed the room to join him.

"Lively company obviously does little to improve your humour, Darcy."

"I cannot tolerate such people. There is not a sincere countenance to be found among them."

"Sincerity, I find, is relative. One cannot ask for what one does not intend to offer."

"Hmph. I suppose you mean to say that because I am guarded, I must accept conniving females in ladies' clothing?"

Fitzwilliam laughed. "Calm yourself, Darcy. We are not here for wives, as you well know. We are here to keep up appearances. I dare say such a stony reception will do little to aid our purpose. Relax. Locate a woman who simpers only half as much as the rest, dance with her, and once I have done the same, we may make our excuses."

Darcy glared at him.

"I do not care for it either," Fitzwilliam sighed, "but we must do our duty."

"Yes, duty indeed," Darcy replied bitterly. The word left a foul aftertaste on his tongue. No longer caring for who he was dancing with, he selected a woman he knew to be considered very eligible. He acquired a dance with Miss Annabelle Peters and led her to the floor, her insufferable blond ringlets bouncing around her shoulders like the boughs of a tree.

"Mr Darcy, we had quite despaired of having your company for the rest of the season! We were sure we

125

were not to see you again until next year at least! I do not wish to be impertinent, but it is said your whole family is absolutely desolate over your cousin's indiscretion. Who knew he could be so very naughty! I know I could scarce believe it when mama related the affair in whole to me. You must have been absolutely humiliated!"

Darcy did not venture a reply, his mouth set in a grim line, and he forced himself to breathe rhythmically as he led Miss Peters around and back again.

"But it is such a treat to be seeing you again, sir! I know several ladies, including myself, who are very glad to see you in such good spirits and dancing again."

Darcy only scowled as he endured her chatter.

"Everyone has been saying that you are all turning him from your doors and have vowed never to see him again! What a calamity this must be! It must be very embarrassing for everyone to know. Were you very mortified?"

"Miss Peters—"

"I do wish there were more such good men as yourself, Mr Darcy. We women are never sure of what sort of

126

man is dancing with us. I know I have danced with your cousin many times in the past, and never knew I was standing up with such an unscrupulous character. It is very difficult to protect oneself, is it not?"

"Yes, I imagine so," he replied simply. He briefly considered mentioning how thankful he was to know she was not permanently blighted from standing up with his "blackguard" cousin, but he held his tongue. Indeed, he had no wish to encourage her into more conversation. To his relief, the set finally ended, and he gratefully returned Miss Peters to her friends. He could not leave her presence quickly enough.

Darcy noticed that his cousin was standing up with another woman, and so he found a corner to hover in. He exhaled unhappily. He had performed his duty this night, and it had definitely been as trying as he had expected.

He thought of Miss Peters in comparison with his Miss Bennet, and he felt physically ill. He could marry Miss Peters tomorrow and everyone would look upon her as a worthy match. It was preposterous in every way. Elizabeth was the woman's superior in understanding, character, decorum, and beauty, yet it was s*he* that would be deemed as unsuitable. Darcy felt disgusted with this world and the role he was obliged to play in it. Elizabeth deserved so much more than Miss Peters would undoubtedly receive. He had no taste for the society or good opinion of these people—it was all superficiality, and it nauseated him. He scarcely waited for his cousin to relinquish his dance partner before departing. Another moment spent in this company was one moment too many.

Chapter Seventeen

March 1812

Elizabeth seated herself on the stone bench overlooking the sea. She had discovered this spot several weeks earlier, less than a mile from Darnwell. It had become her place to escape for hours without being disturbed. Before her lay the wide mouth of the ocean. It went as far as the eye could see, swallowing up the horizon. She had always thought the air was different near the ocean. Fresher, saltier, cooler—it had always seemed to fill the places in her lungs that the inland air could never reach.

As she looked out over its expansive plain, she marvelled at how small she felt, how miniscule…how alone. How hollow she felt! It was difficult for her to swallow, as her throat thickened when she thought of all that had been lost—of all she had never had. She had found a man that understood her without speaking—knew her. A man that she had truly loved for his goodness and for all of his faults. She had given him her heart without him asking, even without her own permission. How she had come to love his closeness, the warmth of his hands, his scent, the way she had felt significant when he spoke to her, how needed she felt when he kissed her! She knew she would have gone through it all again to have back that joy, that lightness of spirit, if only for a little while.

As much as Elizabeth loved her sister, and truly believed that Jane had gotten the happiness she deserved, there were times where she felt wicked and jealous. She could not help but wonder why some people could only have a taste of things that others were given for a lifetime. Her heart felt swollen, and she was sure it did not go on as it had done before. It throbbed instead of beat. The wound it was given had become infected, as though her soul withered from the inside out. No, she would never heal, not when she was paralyzed with the knowledge that she would never feel again for another what she felt for Darcy.

There would never be another creature in the world like him. She would have to be content that he had loved her once. Even if she must accept that happiness would never be hers, she could not blame him for his choice. If anything, she found his selflessness for his sister's sake admirable, even if it meant she would pine for him here, at the edge of all she had ever known. Here, where the land met the sea and the ocean absorbed her tears. In a gulf before her lay her future, an abyss divided her from her past, yet her broken heart remained somewhere in between.

A breeze blew in with the crashing of waves. Elizabeth shivered and pulled her shawl around her, knowing that it was almost time to go in. Though she had never been subjected to such cold winters in Hertfordshire, before that moment she had scarcely noticed. The bone-chilling reality of what had been lost had quite outweighed the coldness of Yorkshire weather. She hated that nothing seemed to matter anymore but her own hurt feelings. Yet, she could not hate them enough to stop examining them. It was a selfish indulgence, but as long as she pined for Darcy, she would not have to let her feelings go. She could grieve the loss of him, and she would not have to laugh for the happiness of others. It was *they* who must understand that she was sad.

It was an unconscious notion that pointed out that no one could truly feel anything for her but worry. Though she did feel guilt, she could not truly open up to them. That would require admitting her own weakness, owning her vulnerability—admitting her rejection. Accepting their pity was something she could not swallow. She was the strong one—the happy, indifferent sister. It hurt too much to say the words because that would make it real, the rejection, the loss—all of it would be real, and she could not bear it, not yet.

Despite the chill and the lateness of hour, she waited there until twilight, for it had become her favourite time of day—when the sky touched the sea and two otherwise separate entities collided, against all odds. She welcomed the ocean spray on her cheeks and watched as the fall of darkness brought the pinks, yellows, and blues that lined the horizon and reflected in the water. The sight was breathtaking, and she remained there, mesmerized by its magnificence. She never wanted to leave.

"Lizzy?"

Elizabeth turned her head at the sound of Charles' voice and noted that he was out of breath.

"Oh, I am so glad to have found you! Jane has been so worried. Have you been sitting here in the rain?"

Elizabeth realized for the first time that it was indeed raining overhead. She had been so consumed by the clear sunset ahead that she had not noticed the clouds above. Belatedly, she determined the ocean spray she had attributed to her wetness was, in fact, rain.

"Lizzy, it is past seven, how long have you been out here?"

"I cannot tell you," she said in confusion. "I believe I must have lost track of time."

"Come," he said, indicating to his horse. "We must get you dry, and Jane is wild for word of you. It was not like you to be away from the house for so long."

"I apologise for worrying you, Charles," Elizabeth said as Bingley helped her on the horse. "It was not intentional, I assure you."

"I am just relieved you are safe and not injured somewhere, as we had feared."

Elizabeth blushed with embarrassment. She was not pleased that her carelessness had worried her sister. But she had not thought—she had not been thinking at all. She was still in a state of shock as Bingley bundled her into the house and into Jane's welcoming arms. As her maid and Jane led her upstairs and stripped her of her wet clothing, Elizabeth said nothing, thinking only of how oblivious she felt to everything. She was very chilled, she knew, but she could not feel it in the usual way. She felt dazed, negligent, and separated from her usual senses. Before she knew it, she was dressed again in warm, dry clothing and wrapped in several shawls. Elizabeth sat on the bed with her sister and apologised profusely for worrying her.

"Nonsense, Lizzy, I am only relieved you are safe. What were you thinking, remaining out in the rain like that?"

"I do not know. I was not myself, I—I was not thinking clearly."

Jane hugged her close. "Do not ever worry me like that again! I was so frightened for you! Do you not know I cannot do without you?"

"Oh, Jane!" Elizabeth sobbed, feeling wretched. She was quite unaware of why she reacted so forcefully, but she clung to her sister and cried, feeling miserable and guilty for causing dear, sweet Jane even the slightest bit of worry. It was irrational, and not entirely to do with the current situation, but Jane did not ask questions. She simply held Elizabeth tightly until she was able to calm herself.

"Dearest, do not make yourself so unhappy. I am not angry, I promise."

"Who am I, Jane?" Elizabeth whispered hoarsely when she had relaxed. "I do not recognize this person."

"You will rally, Lizzy. You always do. There will be happiness again."

"I do not see how," Elizabeth sniffled, her cheek against the mattress as she stared at the wall.

"Have faith."

Elizabeth trembled as she whispered, "Jane?"

"Yes?"

"If you are able, I need you to have faith for me, for I seem to have lost mine."

Chapter Eighteen

"Come away from the fire, dearest," Jane asked Elizabeth gently. Since childhood, Elizabeth had had the misfortune of excessive exposure to the heat of fire bringing on illness. Indeed, it worried Jane to see the intense redness in her sister's cheeks. "Are you too warm?"

Elizabeth smiled when Jane laid the back of her hand against her forehead. "I am well, Jane."

The Bingleys were still struggling to warm their new house against the cold winter outside. Darnwell was a very comfortable estate, but it had gone so long uninhabited that warming it was still a challenge. Elizabeth shivered and pulled her shawl up around her shoulders.

"Shall you be content here?" Jane asked after a small silence.

"I should be content anywhere. However, here with you, my dear sister, I will be happy."

Jane watched her sister closely. Elizabeth looked up when she felt her Jane's gaze upon her.

"Truly, Jane. You need not worry for me. I am perfectly content."

"Lizzy—"

"Jane, please."

"When will you tell me what has happened to you?"

"I told you everything it was necessary for you to know."

"Why must you only keep your own counsel? Have you no confidence in me?"

Elizabeth's expression softened. "I hope you do not truly believe so. If there were something to tell, you would be the first to hear it. Truly, it is nothing but disappointed hopes. Like anything else, they shall run their course, and we will be as we always were."

Jane's brow furrowed, and she wished dearly that she could shake her sister into compliance. "You are unhappy, Lizzy."

"I am perfectly well. I am comfortably situated with my sister at my side. I have the daily pleasure of seeing how Charles dotes on you. I have nothing to want for in my living situation."

"I do not like how flushed your cheeks are," Jane said worriedly. "You ought to go to bed. I hope it is only fatigue that has you looking so."

"If I tell you, you mustn't worry."

"What?" Jane said, leaving her seat to feel Elizabeth's forehead again.

"My head aches and my throat is very sore."

"Let me help you upstairs, Lizzy. I should really wring your neck for allowing yourself to be wet-through tonight."

Elizabeth's lips twitched at the reprimand, but she obeyed. She was asleep before her head hit the pillow.

"People do not die of colds," Elizabeth sniffled as she lay in her bed the following evening. Jane had not permitted her to travel farther than the chamber pot since the evening before—not that she had tried. She had become very content simply to lie with her eyes closed. Her sore throat and fever permitted her to escape into her own thoughts again. She felt that her body and her mind were finally in agreement—all was not well.

"Colds do get worse if not seen to," Jane argued, pressing a cold cloth to Elizabeth's cheeks. "After this has taken its course, you must promise me to take better care of your health."

Elizabeth smiled briefly, but did not respond. The cool cloth felt good against her cheeks, and she drifted off into a dreamless sleep, basking in the comfort of her sister's closeness.

٭

Darcy pressed the handkerchief to his nose. In its fabric it held Elizabeth's tears, tears that fell for him—for them. He had rescued it many a times from the valet, desperate to keep everything he owned as tidy as possible. Months ago it had smelled like her, the scent of Elizabeth's innocent sweetness. How he mourned the loss of her, how he mourned the memory of her pain... how mortified he was with himself! The pain he felt was heightened in the wake of his own mistakes. He had sworn never to injure a woman on his behalf, and Elizabeth had not deserved to be turned away, her heart broken. He had helped, nay, *led* her to love him. Her devastated tears reminded him too much of Georgiana's after the painful transgression she had endured the summer before. He was no better than Wickham.

Despite the certainty of the rightness of his decision, it did not change that he had become a man he could no longer bear to see reflected back in the mirror. What was duty to love? Why must it feel so wrong to walk away from the woman he loved, when every notion of obligation and propriety insisted that it was right? It was clear now, that he had never been worthy of Elizabeth's esteem, never worthy of her love or her tears. He wished he could find a way to cease this feeling that tormented him day and night. He had thought she would have left his mind by now, he had hoped the intensity of regret would wane with time, and that it would get easier. Yet, what he found was that his attachment to Elizabeth had roots too deep to pull.

The futile attempts he had made to put all of this out of his mind and focus on his familial duty had backfired miserably. The women he encountered disgusted him, he cared nothing for visiting his club, or to be seen out amongst the *ton*. Nothing changed the deep ache that had settled in his chest and refused to abate. He was miserable, forlorn, and boorishly unpleasant to be around. His sister continued to avoid him, and his cousin came and went from him as quickly as possible. Any moment open to fill the air left them susceptible to his irritation. Indeed, he would have been content to see no one at all, but that was not to be. There were obligations to be met, expectations for him. He was interrupted from his gloom by the expected knock on his study door. Yet again, his cousin had requested an audience with him—Darcy hoped that this interview

142

would be brief and to the point like so many were between them now.

"I think we had ought to forego our visit to Lady Catherine this year, Darcy," Colonel Fitzwilliam said, coming to stand in the window of Darcy's study.

Darcy was wearily seated in one of his wing-backed chairs, his elbows resting on his knees.

"Considering that every suggestion you have is unpleasant, I imagine you have another idea in mind for travelling."

"I believe it would be right to visit our Gregory and this wife—we must make it known that we are not at odds."

"And how do you intend to make this known?"

"My mother and father will take care of the details. It is you and I that must do the visiting. My mother still cannot tolerate such an expedition for herself."

"So you and I must travel to Rosemont House and visit the viscount and his very scandalous wife."

"I own that this is my plan."

"You are aware I do not find this scheme to my liking."

"I was aware of how you would perceive it, yes."

"And yet you knew I would agree."

The colonel chuckled mirthlessly. "I had that suspicion."

"When are we to go?"

"In April if that is convenient."

Darcy nodded. "And will this be the very last obligation I am expected to perform in respect to this marriage?"

Fitzwilliam sighed and pinched the bridge of his nose, "G-d, I hope so."

"I am convinced she is not even trying to recover," Jane said to Charles that evening as they lay together in bed. "I do not know what to do."

Jane closed her eyes as her husband's gentle fingers ran through her hair soothingly. "It is only a sore throat, and her fever is mild, I should imagine she will recover, whether she wishes or not."

"I have heard of people dying because they do not care to help themselves."

"Yes, my love, but one must be in the position to die before that becomes a concern. I have never heard of a sore throat escalating into anything life threatening."

"But fever can."

"Jane."

"She was never like this until now. Lizzy was a happy girl—she would have laughed to think of someone making themselves ill so carelessly."

"I do not think either of them meant to fall in love," Bingley whispered thoughtfully. "It is a shame his cousin's marriage was so ill-timed."

"I cannot forgive him. If he loved her as she deserves—"

"Yes," Bingley said sadly. "And yet it cannot be easy for either of them."

Jane held her tongue. She did not wish to give her husband pain, but she was still angry over Mr Darcy's treatment of her sister. True, Elizabeth held her share of the responsibility, but it was painful for Jane to see her so unhappy. In her eyes, Mr Darcy was older, educated, and a man of the world. He should have been the better master of himself—he should not have reduced her sister to her current state of despair. It was his responsibility to have acted differently. Now, because he had not, Elizabeth lay in her chamber, barely recognizable as the laughing sister she had always loved. Because of her nature, she found it within herself to pity him and what he must be suffering, however, Jane was not ready to forgive him, and she vowed she would not. Until she could see true smiles in the eyes of her sister again, she could not clear Mr Darcy's name, not even for her husband's sake. She eventually fell into a light sleep, restless worry for her sister leaving her tossing and turning for most of the night.

Chapter Nineteen

The Viscount of Rosemont and his wife, Lady Rosemont, were waiting outside to greet Mr Darcy and Colonel Fitzwilliam as they arrived. Darcy immediately took in the appearance of his infamous new cousin. Lady Rosemont appeared to be attractive, though not exceedingly so, and Darcy could not perceive anything extraordinary in the lady's figure that might have induced such a determination in his cousin to marry her.

Rosemont, like his younger brother, was amiable without being foolish, and was more disposed to smiles than solemnity. He shook hands with both gentlemen and introduced his wife, who to Darcy's surprise, was very quiet and well-mannered. After the usual greetings were given, they all adjourned to the house where the guests were permitted to freshen up before supper.

The meal was a modestly comfortable affair, and Darcy left the conversation to his cousins, preferring to simply observe. It was quickly ascertained that they had been the first to visit the couple since their marriage, and Lady Rosemont was rather nervous over her role as hostess.

"Have you spent the winter in Town then, Darcy?" Rosemont asked, drawing his cousin from his silent thoughts.

"Yes, I had thought it best this year."

He noted that Lady Rosemont immediately coloured at this response, and her hand was covered by her husband's. Darcy had not meant to draw attention to the obvious upset they had endured this winter, and now he could not think of an appropriate way to smooth things over. Fortunately, Richard was not so unlucky.

"The north experienced a particularly chilly winter this year, Brother, and so Darcy and I thought it best to stay warm in Town."

148

"I am sure Georgiana had no complaints with that plan," Rosemont smiled.

"Ana is simply content to be where her brother is, I think," Fitzwilliam replied.

Darcy finally found his voice, "I would not have you think she requires me, in fact, of late, I think she is content to be relieved of her overly serious brother."

"She is very lucky to have you," Lady Rosemont said, speaking for the first time since they were seated. "I always longed for a sibling."

"Yes, Lillian, that is what everyone says until said sibling is pestering and fighting with them incessantly, is it not, Brother?"

Colonel Fitzwilliam laughed. "Your husband and I had our share of scrapes and disagreements, madam. We caused my mother and father an intolerable amount of grief and vexation."

"Not to mention your poor cousins," Darcy replied.

"Lily, Darcy would have you believe he was not a party to most of our indiscretions, but it is a well known fact that he instigated his fair share. Do not let his current severity fool you. There was a time when he helped his

149

cousins with plenty of mischief. He was too clever for us by half."

"Little has changed, you see," Colonel Fitzwilliam laughed. The rest of the meal was spent recounting childhood stories for the amusement of Lady Rosemont. Darcy could not help but relax with her manners, for she was very genteel, and her comportment was flawless. Soon, supper was completed, and catching her husband's eye, Lady Rosemont excused herself to leave the men to their port.

"You cannot know how thankful I am that you chose to visit us. We have not sought anyone's approval, but Lillian has been troubled that she has caused a rift amongst family. It was a relief to have my family visit."

"Brother, you know that we are family before anything. We would not forgo visiting your wife, no matter the scandal in Town."

"But I imagine that this is also an attempt to prove us to be united as a family. Father would not have us appear at odds, of course."

"No," Darcy said. "My uncle has always concentrated on keeping his family respectable."

"At any cost," Rosemont laughed. "I am no fool, Darcy. I know this winter has been spent rectifying the damage I have caused by my marriage."

Darcy did not speak.

"It has not been easy," Fitzwilliam owned. "The gossip pages have not been kind."

"No, I imagine not."

The colonel sighed. "I will not relate to you all that has been said, but—"

"But it has been my wife who bears the brunt of their attacks," Rosemont finished for him. "Insufferable, the lot of them."

"You could not have thought it would have ended otherwise?" Darcy said rather unkindly. "You are the heir to a well-respected earl, Rosemont! Your wife has no father at all!"

"Lower your voice," Rosemont said evenly. "I do not care to have Lillian overhear our conversation. She does not deserve your disdain; it is I who have disappointed you."

"Indeed it is," Darcy said gravely. Rosemont shook his head.

"But in time it will be forgot," Colonel Fitzwilliam offered, "and your wife seems to be well-mannered enough to comport herself respectably for any occasion. I believe, despite our difference in opinion, we would all like to see her eventually accepted as a worthy lady."

"Yes," Rosemont sighed. "Though I will not expose her to the disdainful remarks of jealous women. Lillian will not be seen in Town for some time, I assure you."

"Perhaps that is for the best," Darcy sighed, and he noticed his cousin's eyes dart toward him angrily.

"You are wrong to judge her, Cousin," Rosemont said quietly. "She is my wife. I offered for *her*, not the other way around."

Darcy did not reply and was relieved when the conversation ended, and they joined Lady Rosemont in the drawing room for more neutral conversation. Before long it was time for bed, and they all made to retire. Darcy was stalled in his progress by a hand coming to rest on his shoulder.

"Darcy, I know you are angry, and no doubt after what you have endured this winter, your feelings are justified," Rosemont said softly, "but there are things that are more important than society's good opinion."

Darcy nodded briefly and eyed his cousin carefully. The viscount seemed to have humbled considerably since they had last seen one another.

"Ride out with me tomorrow, I have a few spots of land I think you would be glad to visit."

"After breakfast then?"

Rosemont smiled and bade him goodnight. Darcy watched his cousin disappear around the corner before turning and entering his own chamber, the events of the day serving to puzzle him exceedingly.

Chapter Twenty

Elizabeth's fever broke less than a day later. Jane's unsolicited care and attention brought about her recovery more quickly than anyone would have expected. That day, Elizabeth was sitting up in her bed, taking some broth brought up to her from the kitchen. Jane had been silent at her bedside for some time, and Elizabeth decided to reassure her sister so that she might see to other things.

"Jane, you surely do not have sit with me. I will be quite well here on my own."

Jane shook her head thoughtfully, but it was several minutes before she replied. "No, you are not well. You have not been well for some time. Even now, you are not *trying* to be well. All of this could have been avoided if you had kept enough sense about you to care for your own health. You have had me worried and frightened for you again and again for months."

Elizabeth was taken aback by her sister's tone. She opened her mouth to speak, but Jane held up her hand.

"I do not want you to say anything, Lizzy. For all you have had to say to me for months is that you are well, and I should not worry. You have nothing of substance to say, you lie to me—if not literally, then by omission. I do not wish to hear another word from your lips until you are willing to be honest with me," Jane finished, her voice caught in a sob.

Elizabeth looked at her hands, ashamed. Jane's words mortified her, and she knew every word of it was true. She turned back to her sister, tears of regret in her eyes.

"I am very glad you are well. Perhaps you might come downstairs tomorrow," Jane said, leaving the room.

Elizabeth watched the doorway a long time, at last thinking of the consequences of her actions. She did not reflect upon her behaviour with any pleasure, and it was clear she owed Jane and Charles so many apologies for repaying their kindness in this way. Tears filled her eyes at the realization. She knew she had to stop this. No, this could not be the rest of her life—she had to make an effort, for herself *and* for her sister. Things could not go on this way.

"A thrown horseshoe," Rosemont said thoughtfully as he looked out into the distance. He and Darcy had ridden out early as planned and had just reached a fine prospect that afforded them a wonderful view of the landscape below.

"What?"

"If it had not been for a thrown horseshoe just outside of London, I might never have met my Lily."

"Mmm," was Darcy's noncommittal reply. He could not help but consider all the great trouble something as simple as a thrown horseshoe had caused.

"Darcy, we have known one another all our lives, and I am fully aware that you resent my decision. You should be fully aware, however, that I am unconcerned with your or any one else's feelings on the matter."

"I believe you have made that abundantly clear, Cousin."

Rosemont turned to inspect his cousin's features, the bitterness in his voice giving him pause.

"Yes, but what is not entirely clear to you, I think, is why I have done what I have."

"You owe me no such explanation."

"Do I not? I would think you anxious to know why a seemingly intelligent gentleman like myself would cast aside all he has been taught is his duty, and dispose of himself in such a way."

"It is not my business to pry into your concerns, Gregory."

"And yet you have taken up my cross to bear."

Darcy continued to stare straight ahead. He had not come to exact answers from his cousin, and he certainly cared nothing for his sympathy.

"I reacted much as I would imagine you did to the idea. I met Lillian, and before I knew myself, I was in love. But it was not enough—she was grievously unsuitable, and I am the heir of a well-respected earl. As would any

157

man in my position, I fought my feelings and did everything in my power to push her away."

"What convinced you otherwise?"

"Love."

Darcy scowled at his hands as they clutched the reins of his horse.

"I finally allowed myself to comprehend that Lily was the woman I loved because of who she is—including her situation in life. Gentlemen like you and I, Darcy, are taught to believe that the women we marry are to compliment our rank, wealth, and connections. She is meant to make yet another ornament to hang about our shoulders—responsibility to our grand estate, our good name, our impressive income, and reputation. It all conceals what really matters, I think."

"Which is?"

"That we are searching for someone who *sees* us...in here," Rosemont said, pressing his hand to his heart. "How many men of our station can say they have a woman who loves him solely for his heart, for the man he is beneath the layers of duty and privilege? How many then can say that this woman would not care if all of his consequence was lost tomorrow?"

Darcy felt the weight of his cousin's gaze, and he turned to look at him.

"I can, Darcy."

"Then you are a very rich man, indeed."

"Darcy, I know you better than most—is this not what you desire?"

Darcy did not venture a reply, as he felt a wave of emotion set in. He suddenly felt very weary.

"You will not find that kind of woman in Town, Cousin. It was difficult for me to accept, as well. Yet, I had to realize that Lillian is the woman I love not in spite of her connections, but because of them. She spent her childhood under the protection of those who taught her to live simply, to be kind, and to look at the character of a man before assessing his riches. She is a true diamond in the rough, and I would have been a fool to let such happiness slip through my fingers. The women in Town are vain, selfish, senseless creatures—I have seen how you look at them, and I share your opinion.

159

"Their minds and hearts are empty, worthless. You search for a wife amongst them, and you will find yourself saddled to a simpering, simpleminded woman you detest with no way of being rid of her. She would bear your children and teach them to be vain and ridiculous like herself—I could not stomach such a future, and thus, chose otherwise. As for the rest, I never asked for any of you to mend what I broke, Darcy. You could have written me off the pages of your lives, and I would have understood. It would have been worth it to me."

Darcy turned his head sharply at this proclamation.

"You think me ungrateful?"

"I confess I do not know what to think."

"Ungrateful, in my eyes, is to be given such a precious treasure and not spend the rest of your life expressing your gratitude that it came your way. Few people ever find such love, Cousin. Who am I to refuse when it is offered to me? Lillian, she breathes life into me."

Darcy did not respond. Such an unsolicited speech from his cousin was chilling. Rosemont could not have known about Elizabeth, of his private struggle, and yet

160

he was advising him as though he did. A coincidence, perhaps, but a significant one.

They rode back in silence, both men lost in thought. As they entered the house, Darcy watched his cousin's wife greet his return as though he had been gone for days instead of hours. The realization hit Darcy in one fell swoop—they *were* in love. So in love, in fact, that they were prepared to face the censure of the world to be together. Unconsciously, his hand reached to his pocket and removed Elizabeth's handkerchief. As his thumb rubbed gently against the fabric, he wondered if the good opinion of the rest of the world was worth anything if he did not have Elizabeth. For the first time, he did not feel so sure.

Chapter Twenty-one

Elizabeth sat by the window, her shawl wrapped around her shoulders, her eyes fixed on an unfocused point in the distance. Jane's words to her the other evening swam in her mind, and she could not forget them. Indeed, if this was to be the only chance she had for life in this world, she would not spend it despairing over what could never be. She could not close herself off from the rest of the world. It was time she accepted that there were people who loved her very much and could be depended upon, if she would only let them. She turned from the window to look at Jane, who sat close to the fire, embroidering a cushion. The sisters met eyes, and Elizabeth shared a smile with Jane. They had not spoken a word to one another for nearly two days. Finally, Elizabeth felt ready to speak, ready to keep going.

Hesitating only a moment, she left her place at the window and seated herself across from Jane. "I *did* have my heart broken, and I *did* stop trying. I am sorry for that, Jane." It was then that Elizabeth related the whole story to her sister, describing how she fell in love with an unattainable man against her will, her disappointment at his leaving, and the devastation she had experienced in London when he told her they could never be together. "I did not want to keep going, and I am afraid I thought only of myself for the longest time. I could not make myself care for the feelings of others—my own hurt feelings quite outweighed any other consideration. It was wrong of me to conceal everything from you, Jane. You deserved more than that. I am genuinely sorry for all the grief and trouble I have caused, and while I do not think it will be easy for me to change my ways, I promise to do better and try harder."

Jane hugged Elizabeth and promised her she was not angry with her—only thankful that the tide had somehow changed. They sat in silence a while longer, both enjoying the return of their closeness.

"Have you opened your letter from my aunt, Lizzy?" Jane asked in a bit.

"Yes," Elizabeth replied, moving to retrieve it from the writing desk there. She passed the letter on to her sister, who took it and read.

Friday, 17 April 1812

Dear Elizabeth,

> *Your uncle finds it within his power to leave London for several weeks. We have decided that, if you are agreeable, you had ought to come with us. We have a mind to tour the countryside, and I would very much like to visit my childhood home in Lambton. Your uncle and I both agree that it would be an excellent thing to have you with us.*
>
> *Jane wrote to us of her concern for you and of the time you spent unwell. She says you will not confide in her. I will not ask you to tell me of your troubles, but I extend the offer if you are inclined to speak of them. Remember, Elizabeth, that we all love you very much.*

164

Mary has written to us, and she speaks favourably of her situation in Kent. One may not write much of her husband's sense, but I wish them very happy. She would have me understand very little goes on at the parsonage. She writes mostly of her husband's sermons and the kindness extended to them by Lady Catherine.

If you are agreeable to joining our expedition, write in the affirmative, and you may expect us to send for you on the second week of June. We will return you to Mrs Bingley the second week in July, before our return to London.

As Jane has expressed a wish of hearing more of my children, be so kind as to mention that they are very well and ask after her regularly. They are to stay with your mother and father while we are away, despite my concerns that their behaviour may be a bit trying for you mother's nerves. Your uncle, as always, sends his love, and we both wish everyone at Darnwell very happy.

I pray that this letter has found you well. Take care, Lizzy, to smile when the sky is blue.

Your devoted aunt,

M. Gardiner

"Do you plan to go, then?"

"I thought I might, if you could bear to spare me," Elizabeth owned.

"I think it a very good plan," Jane said seriously, returning the letter to Elizabeth's hands. "You would have a lovely time, I am sure, and you would benefit from the warmer weather, I think."

"I would not have my sisters think Mr and Mrs Gardiner favour me."

"Nonsense, Kitty and Lydia would think it a punishment to be visiting old houses in the summertime."

"You are right," Elizabeth sighed. "I confess I would very much like to go."

"Then it is settled," Jane said seriously. "You must write to my aunt this afternoon, accepting her invitation."

Elizabeth laughed at Jane's impulsiveness, but took her advice. It was soon determined that she would travel with the Gardiners in June, and Elizabeth concentrated on spending her time before then lifting her spirits. If she had no intention of being anything more than sister, niece, or daughter to anyone, she would make the most of it.

True to her word, Elizabeth did try, and she rallied considerably in the two months that followed. Elizabeth had always been better suited for happiness than grief, and so she set her sights on reminding herself of one thing she could be thankful for each day. Yes, her heart had certainly been broken, but she could not simply stop living. Nothing was ever so bad as that.

∾

Darcy and Colonel Fitzwilliam spent nearly four weeks with the viscount and his wife. Darcy could not help but envy the happiness he had finally admitted existed between the couple. It had occurred to him, during that time, that perhaps not everything ought to be weighed by how it would be received by the *ton*. Every day, in his pocket, he kept the handkerchief that symbolized Elizabeth's love—it had become both a yoke and a treasure.

They left their cousins in the beginning of May, Colonel Fitzwilliam travelling to Desham with the intent of reporting his brother's condition to his parents, and Darcy returning to his sister in London. He had decided that it was perhaps time to ask Georgiana's opinions on this entire matter. Darcy suspected that she might be capable of shining a new light on this subject that had been plaguing him for months. Most importantly, she undoubtedly would be able to tell him if he had done right—for he was honestly beginning to lose faith that he had.

Chapter Twenty-two

"And so this is what has had you so agitated," Georgiana said softly. She looked to her brother, who stood at the mantel, breathing heavily. He always seemed to breathe harder when he was emotional. She had not expected him to open up to her in this way. Darcy almost never shared his concerns with her, preferring always to keep his own counsel. It had surprised her significantly when he had arrived that morning anxious to tell her everything. Even now, she struggled to comprehend the whole of it.

"What I do not understand then, is what Gregory has to do with Miss Bennet."

Darcy smiled, but she knew he was not at all amused. "At once, he has everything and nothing to do with Miss Bennet."

Georgiana waited. She needed more information. Finally, Darcy came and seated himself beside her. She offered him her hand. "I determined I could not marry her because of what had happened with Gregory."

"Yes, you said that."

"The whole notion is preposterous, is it not? My cousin makes the indiscretion, I choose to do what is right, and yet who is punished? It surely is not him, for I have never seen two people more happily married."

Georgiana sat quietly, her brow furrowed in confusion. In a moment, she looked at her brother to see him watching her. "What you have suffered!" she said feelingly.

"Ana, I ask you to tell me. Have I chosen wisely? I feel as though my perspective has been lost, I hardly know myself these days."

She could see by his movements he was very agitated, and she had to look away to concentrate on forming an answer. Georgiana had learned a very painful lesson by attempting to follow her own heart the summer before when George Wickham, a disgraced family friend, had taken advantage of her naivety and convinced her that she was in love with him, and she had agreed to an elopement. If her brother had not happened upon them on the eve of their departure, she knew now she would have been lost to him forever. Even the thought now sent chills down her spine. How close she had come to losing everything she held dear! An entire year had not lessened the mortification she felt at her own lack of perception. Hence, Georgiana was frightened even to suggest that her brother follow his own heart. Why would he ask her feelings? Did he attempt to query her understanding on what was proper?

"All signs of propriety would suggest that you have indeed done what is right and good. I know you could never do anything that was not. You acted to protect our family from further shame. I am sure you did what you knew you must. You never behave rashly. It grieves me to think you suffer for it," she replied almost mechanically.

She saw her brother look at her in sadness, and her stomach clenched. Had her answer displeased him?

"I beseech you, Ana, do not tell me what you think I wish to hear. I come to you today to beg your honesty. I

171

will think no less of you for expressing the truth of your feelings."

"I am honoured by your confidence in me, but do you not think that I am an unsuitable counsel for this particular struggle? Have I not completely displayed my unworthiness to judge properly in matters of the heart?"

"No, you have not," he replied emphatically. "You cannot always blame yourself for a youthful indiscretion."

"It was *not* a mere youthful indiscretion, Fitzwilliam. I nearly threw everything away for a deceptive fantasy."

"You were deceived by one acting a part, and you learned a painful lesson. If there is anyone more suitable to speak sensibly on this matter, I ask you to show them to me at once, for I can think of no better than you."

She remained quiet as she mulled over his speech. "Truthfully?" she finally asked softly.

"I beg it of your justice."

"If I have learned anything, it is that those who truly love us come as a precious few."

Darcy's mouth pursed grimly. "Indeed."

"Particularly for us, who have only one another."

"That very much echoes what Gregory has said."

Georgiana hesitated. "I—" she faltered and closed her mouth, thinking again before deciding to speak her mind. "Brother, you could be happy, too. What do you care for society's favour?"

"I have not only myself to think of."

"It sounds as though Miss Bennet would not care one way or the other as long as you were together."

"No, I daresay she would not." Darcy squeezed her hand. "But it is you I was talking of, Ana."

"Me? Brother, I fail to comprehend what this has to do with me."

"Your name is inevitably affected by my actions. How could I act, and know it would jeopardize your prospects of marrying well?"

"Fitzwilliam, do I seem to you the kind of person who aspires to be the next society darling? Have I ever once reminded you of Miss Bingley? In any case, it should be years before I consider marrying, if I consider it at all," Georgiana said gently. "I learned with disturbing clarity last summer that I am not at all prepared for the attentions of any man."

"I would not have my actions make things more difficult for you. There would be some who would rule out a connection with you based upon who your brother chooses for his wife."

"And there will be some who will be more interested in my dowry than in me," she finished for him. "Neither of them would produce an ideal husband in any case. If a man is discouraged by anything so wholly unrelated to the woman I will be, then I would beg you to marry Miss Bennet for that benefit alone. I wish to marry for love, and nothing else. The kind of gentleman I could love would not calculate my worth based upon the actions of my relatives."

Darcy did not reply, and Georgiana felt for him. He was deeply troubled, his brow creased fiercely and his shoulders slumped. She did the only thing she knew to do, and wrapped her arms around him. He held her tightly, something he usually did when he was particularly worried or concerned—usually for her. But he was not the concerned sibling today, it was she who felt the overwhelming need to protect him and insist he be happy.

"Brother, if you love her, I beg you to follow your heart. You deserve to be happy, and you have done your duty to us all. You take care of everyone, and yet no one takes care of you. I want so much to look after you, but as a younger sister, I know you cannot always let me. If she loves you as you say, then I have faith that she will see that you never want for anything. You cannot always be protecting the rest of us. If you had done right you would not be so unhappy."

"I came here convinced you would see the merits of my choosing as I have."

"I gave you that answer, and it was not to your liking."

"The insincerity in your voice grieved me. I knew you were only attempting to respond with what you believed I wanted you to say. Ana, I could not live with myself if you suffered from my actions."

"Fitzwilliam, you worry too much. You will have frown lines before long," she said, running her fingers soothingly along his forehead.

Darcy gave her a small smile. "You truly think I have done wrong?"

"I think you ought to cease worrying about everyone else, and think of your own needs, just this once. If my cousin is indeed so very happy, perhaps you might take a cue from him."

"What did you think of Miss Bennet when you met her?"

"I thought she was lovely, if a bit sad about the eyes. Her sister, aunt, and uncle were very kind; I found nothing wanting with any of them. Miss Elizabeth Bennet, I confess, *was* my favourite. She makes you feel so comfortable in her presence even though you have only just met."

"A gift neither of us possesses, I am afraid."

"No," Georgiana smiled. "But it is possible if she came to live with us we might learn...I believe."

Darcy gave her a surprised look, and she gave his hand a firm squeeze as she rose to leave the room.

"Think on it, Brother, surely there can be no harm in that."

Chapter Twenty-three

The month of May passed quickly, and soon enough Elizabeth found herself travelling with the Gardiners. Although one can never return to the way they were before their first heartbreak, Elizabeth had recovered steadily in the passing months, and learned not to think so much on the things that she could not change. She had eventually ventured out and made several friends in the small town just outside of Darnwell. Though several men had paid her attentions, she found she could still not abide them—she just was not ready to begin again, there was still more healing to be had. It had been a long winter, and with the sunshine came a return of her smiles and laughter. She was again feeling like herself, the Lizzy everyone loved—and when she was sure no one was watching, she would travel down to the ocean and curl her toes in the water that washed up on the sand.

When she greeted her aunt and uncle again, she was able to welcome them with her familiar bright smile, and they spent a long while in the carriage catching up on the events of their lives in the time they had spent apart. The route to Derbyshire, where they travelled to Lambton, was lined with fine enough estates to keep Elizabeth's mind occupied agreeably for the journey. Her quick eyes and ready mind took in all there was to see and learn. They finally arrived in Lambton near the end of June. Over supper that evening, Mrs Gardiner posed the question that Elizabeth had all along known to be inevitable, as Pemberley was not five miles from their current location.

"We could not be so near Pemberley without my asking, Lizzy. Would you not like to see this great house of which you have heard so much?"

"I should think it would be very awkward for us to be there without an invitation."

"No more than anywhere else we have seen," her uncle reasoned.

"Lizzy, the family is not likely to be home this time of year."

Elizabeth felt torn. Could she truly visit Pemberley? "Do you really wish it, aunt?"

"I had thought *you* would be more anxious to see it."

Elizabeth did not reply. She was worried that Pemberley would remind her too much of its owner. She did not think she could bear feeling such sadness again. On the other hand, she was curious to see Pemberley's beauty for herself. Mr Darcy had often spoken so highly of the place, that it would have been unnatural for her not to wish to see it. She reasoned that this might be the last thing she needed before she could truly move on. Perhaps it would complete the picture in her mind's eye of the man she had come to admire so greatly. Indeed, after all that had happened, she still thought him to be the best man she had ever known.

"If you are confident that we shall not encounter the family, I shall not resist," she said at last.

"Well, then," Mrs Gardiner smiled. "Shall we go tomorrow?"

"Tomorrow is as good as any day, I think," her husband said cheerfully. "What do you say, Lizzy?"

"Tomorrow then," she said thoughtfully.

∾◌∾

Darcy could feel the grime that had accumulated on his face and body as he rode toward Pemberley. He and Georgiana had agreed upon spending the remainder of the summer there, though his own impatience had sent him riding ahead of his sister and her companion. After perhaps the longest winter of his life, Darcy was greatly looking forward to the solace only Pemberley could offer. He had mulled over his actions, and the actions of others, again and again, only to realize there was no right answer to be handed to him. He alone would have to determine what was best. That, of course, was much easier said than done.

He arrived at Pemberley and travelled directly to the stables where he abandoned his horse. Feeling the layer of dust and sweat drying on his skin, he considered

180

diving into the lake that was located around the side of the house, but decided against it. Instead, he walked indoors, and up to his bedchamber without encountering anyone. Exhausted, but thankful to be home, he lay down on the bed and promptly fell asleep.

✿

Elizabeth found Pemberley to be absolutely breathtaking. The landscape that surrounded it spread out in rich colours of green as far as the eye could see. She immediately discerned that Mr Darcy was in no way exaggerating in his praise of the estate. It was beautiful, and she was required to remind herself to close her mouth on more than one occasion. Mrs Reynolds, the housekeeper, was found to be a very kind, elderly woman, and she welcomed them sincerely as she ushered them inside.

Elizabeth thought of inquiring if Mr Darcy was truly from home, but she was afraid to do so, lest they be told he was not. She was spared of the task, however, by her uncle, who asked after him.

181

"Indeed, he is not. However, we expect him and Miss Darcy later in the week. We are very glad to have them back as they have been in Town almost exclusively for the winter and spring."

Elizabeth puffed her cheeks, and thanked heaven they had not thought to delay even a day in their travels. Even so, she could not relax herself, as she quite expected Mr Darcy to come around some corner or another at every moment. They were led through several rooms on the ground floor, and Elizabeth drank in every detail. Eventually they came to stand in front of a portrait of Miss Darcy, and she paused, admiring how very much alike brother and sister were in appearance.

"That is Miss Darcy, there," Mrs Reynolds explained. "My master had that painted of her this year, and it has only just arrived. She is a beautiful young lady, if I do say so."

"Indeed she is," Mrs Gardiner agreed.

"If you will come with me," Mrs Reynolds began, "I will take you upstairs to see a portrait of the master. It is only two years old, and very like him."

182

"Well, what do you think of Pemberley?" Mrs Gardiner whispered to Elizabeth as they followed the housekeeper upstairs.

"Undeniably charming," she replied quietly. "I can easily see why its owner is so fond of it."

"There!" Mrs Reynolds exclaimed, stopping at a very large portrait hung in the hallway. "Is he not the handsomest gentleman you have ever seen?"

"Yes," Elizabeth whispered, a reply heard only by herself. She found that if she stood just so, the man in the portrait seemed to look directly at her. It was a lovely portrait, and she determined that his gentle expression was one she had seen often during his time in Hertfordshire. He was beautiful, she could never deny that, and it would have been impossible for her heart not to ache at the sight of him. After a few moments, she turned away and walked to the window to calm herself. Mrs Reynolds must have led her aunt and uncle further up the hall, for she heard their voices travel away from her.

As she looked out at the landscape surrounding the house, she felt her heart jump. What would it feel like to be mistress of all this? To look out these windows upon this great land as her own? There was no disputing why Mr. Darcy was so fond of this place. It was beyond comparison to any of the great houses they had visited in their travels. None had the wildness of untamed nature permitted to flourish as did Pemberley. She sighed, but that was not the rarest treasure that Pemberley had to offer. The house and lands were very fine, exceptionally so, yet it was the master that was the true prize. In her eyes, there was no equal.

It was perhaps not well done to come here, she reasoned emotionally. Elizabeth had been fighting tears valiantly for the better part of the afternoon. She knew herself to be very flushed, and she took several very deep breaths to calm the jittering panic she felt to be among the very spirit of the man she loved. The walls, the foundation, the trees, the water—they all breathed of him, like cords irrevocably intertwined. Closing her eyes, she focused on another thought—of carriage wheels and long dusty roads—anything to distract herself from the predicament she now found herself in. When she was calm enough, she joined her party again, and Mrs

184

Reynolds led them back outside where they were entrusted with the gardener there, and led away to explore the grounds.

⚬

Darcy awoke from his nap several hours later, and determined it to be later in the afternoon. Groggily, he pulled the cord for assistance, though he noticed that it was some time before a person came in response.

"Master!" Mrs Reynolds cried in surprise when she saw him. "I thought it must have been my imagination when I heard the ring. Have you been up here all this time?"

"The fault is mine, I did not notify anyone of my arrival, and simply came upstairs and fell asleep. I believe I have been sleeping since noon."

"I suppose that is fortunate, sir. As I was giving some travellers a tour of the house during that time."

"Ah," Darcy said, thankful he had missed them. "If you could please send someone up to prepare a bath, I would be eternally grateful. I thoughtlessly dirtied the bed covers when I arrived. I fear I was too exhausted to consider the state of myself before lying down."

"Never you mind, sir. It will be seen to," Mrs Reynolds smiled. "I am very glad to have you home with us, Mr Darcy."

Darcy smiled back at the sweet lady who had been like a mother to him for as long as he could remember. It was indeed good to be home.

Once he had bathed and dressed, Darcy came downstairs to the library. He buried himself in the business neglected during his long winter in London. After a while, though, he grew weary of it and strode over to look out the window. Georgiana would be there soon, and the house would not seem quite so quiet. At least she would provide a little music and conversation. When he was alone like this, he found he could only think of Elizabeth.

He knew now, that if he had had it all to do over again, it was possible that he would have chosen differently. This honour, this obligation he had felt for his family had not been worth losing her. He felt, however, that it was much too late now to change his mind—she had undoubtedly moved on. He reached to his pocket and pulled out the handkerchief. Months had passed, removing from it the remnants of Elizabeth that he had come to treasure. Now, only the memory of her tears, long dried in that small piece of fabric, remained. No, he had not chosen right.

Despite his ruminations, his eye caught on some people below, near the lake. He watched them for a moment with passive curiosity. However, when the woman turned around, he absolutely started. Surely his eyes were deceiving him! It could not possibly be—

"Mrs Reynolds!" he called, striding out into the hallway.

"Sir?"

"Do you recall the names of your travellers from this afternoon?"

Mrs Reynolds appeared to think very hard. "Gardiner, perhaps? Why do you ask?"

"Never mind, thank you," he said, hurrying away. He had dashed out the door and down the front stairs, still unable to believe what his eyes were telling him was true. It was unbelievable that he had seen Elizabeth, yet he would have known her anywhere. It simply could not be anyone else. He forced himself to walk, though it was as quickly as possible, toward the guests who had now been led even farther away on the property. A moment later, and he might have never seen them from the window.

"Mr Darcy," the gardener said with surprise to see his master approaching.

Darcy watched as Elizabeth whirled around, her eyes wide. It was clear none of them had expected to see him this day. He noted that she blushed violently, but he could not take his eyes from her. How or why she had come to Pemberley was the farthest thing from his thoughts at that moment, for he was beyond thankful to see her.

"Mr Darcy," she said, with a curtsey.

"A pleasure to see you, Miss Bennet."

Mr Gardiner and his wife both expressed their gladness in seeing him. Darcy spoke to them very briefly, and was able to perceive that this was one stop of many scheduled for their travels. He expressed his pleasure that they had chosen to view Pemberley.

"We would not have dreamed of doing so had we known you were to be here, sir," Elizabeth said uneasily.

"It is no fault of yours, it was I who returned ahead of schedule," he said, hurrying to comfort her.

Darcy ascertained what remained of the tour from the gardener, and dismissed him back to his work. He then led his guests the rest of the way. He noticed Elizabeth was uncharacteristically silent, and kept an eye on her always. She seemed greatly troubled by meeting him again, and he regretted being the cause of her discomfort. Nevertheless, she seemed even more beautiful to him than he remembered and he had to force himself to concentrate on the conversation he held with Mr Gardiner. Too soon, the tour was over, and despite his offer, his guests were not willing to go back inside for refreshments. He was forced then to hand Elizabeth into her uncle's carriage without the opportunity of conversing with her.

As the horses pulled them away from Pemberley, Elizabeth could feel herself trembling, and endeavoured to calm her breathing. Seeing Mr Darcy after all had given her the shock of her life, and she was too mortified for words. What he must think of her coming to his home after all that had passed between them? It had been foolish indeed coming there, and she cursed the bad luck of his arriving early.

"Uncle?" Elizabeth asked, her voice shaky.

"Mmm?"

"How far is our next destination?"

"Not above two hours, I believe."

"Is it possible that we may go that way today instead of tomorrow? The day is young yet."

"Tonight?" Mrs Gardiner said, surprised. "What has caused such an anxiousness to leave?"

Momentarily, she attempted to find an excuse, but she recalled her determination to no longer conceal her discomfort from those she loved.

"It is too much," Elizabeth replied, trying desperately not to cry. "I thought I could manage to see his house, but it is too much to see him again. I am so mortified! What must he think of me?"

"There, there, my dear," Mrs Gardiner said gently, wrapping an arm around her niece. "He did not seem so very cross to see you. But we may go, if it gives you comfort."

"Yes, I do not see why that cannot be managed," Mr Gardiner agreed solemnly.

Elizabeth nodded, and a tear slipped down her cheek. Seeing Darcy again had seemed to liberate the stream of emotions she had worked so diligently to cut off. He had appeared so tired, so weary, and it pained her to see him so. Even then, he had to have been regretting her reappearance in his life. *She* regretted it, they should never have presumed to come. In her mind, they could not leave quickly enough.

Chapter Twenty-Four

Darcy returned to the house highly agitated. The emotions in his breast threatened to undo him, and he had certainly just experienced the greatest shock of his life in seeing Elizabeth at Pemberley. Seeing her again evoked an energy within him, and he paced the length of the library anxiously. One thing was certain, he was still deeply in love with her. The thought of her going away again unnerved him. He did not know what to do with himself, and he did not like to be impulsive. He considered following her; he knew he ought to have tried more to speak with her, but his love for her left him speechless in her presence. Elizabeth belonged at Pemberley, it was a feeling he felt deep in his bones. This was meant to be her home, and he could not possibly imagine another woman taking her place.

Suddenly, he was reminded of something Rosemont had said.

"Ungrateful, in my eyes, is to be given such a precious treasure and not spend the rest of your life expressing your gratitude that it came your way. Few people ever find such love…"

Instantly, he knew what was right, and knew exactly what was left for him to do. Indeed he could think of nothing else after such an epiphany. He rushed into the hallway and shouted for his horse to be readied.

He rode into Lambton fiercely, thankful his man had thought to give him a different horse than was his usual animal, the other likely unable to endure his impatience after only just arriving from his previous journey. Indeed, he knew he was being very reckless by riding much too fast, but he could not calm himself. He had decided on one possible course of action, and he could not wait a moment longer than necessary to see it through. He had discerned from the uncle where they were staying, and he dismounted quickly, striding inside purposefully.

"Hello there. I am here to see a Mr Gardiner, can you take me to him?"

"Oh no, sir, Mr Gardiner and his party have left an hour ago at least."

Darcy frowned. "Are you absolutely certain? Mr Gardiner does not intend on coming back?"

"No, sir. Seen 'em leavin' with their belongings, I did."

Darcy cursed under his breath. "Thank you," he said tightly as he strode back out. He looked left and right, trying to discern which way they might have gone. At last making a decision, he climbed back astride his horse and rode fiercely down the road. He knew he would feel extremely foolish if they had not gone this way, but he was almost positive that they had. He pushed the horse hard for half an hour before he was forced to ease up on it. Darcy continually promised himself that just around one corner or at the top of the next hill he would find them.

At last, when he began to doubt he would, he saw a carriage in the distance. When he got up to it, he took his riding crop and banged it against the side. At first, the driver appeared alarmed and prepared to pull his gun out, but Darcy's appearance evidently convinced him that he was a gentleman, and the carriage stopped so that Darcy could look inside. Indeed, it was them, and he closed his eyes for a moment in relief. He opened them to see each inhabitant of the carriage watching him with alarmed expectancy.

"Forgive me for frightening you. I came into Lambton and discovered you had gone away. I simply could not allow you to go," he said, looking only at Elizabeth.

"Is there something amiss?" Mr Gardiner queried.

"Yes," Darcy replied after he had dismounted, "If you would permit me to speak privately with your niece, sir, perhaps it might be rectified."

Mr Gardiner looked from Darcy to Elizabeth in confusion. "Pardon me, sir, do you mean now?"

"Yes, please, Mr Gardiner."

"Lizzy?" her uncle asked, and she nodded, though reluctantly, and allowed Darcy to hand her down. He led her around to stand behind the carriage, never releasing her hands. He looked into her eyes for several moments, realizing that he had forgotten to think of what he meant to say to her in his haste.

"Miss Bennet, Elizabeth, how do I even begin again after what has passed between us?" he said softly. "I dare not believe your feelings are unchanged, but if by some fantastic chance they are what they were before, I must ask you what I should have asked you last November."

Darcy paused to take in her expression, and saw that tears had welled in her eyes. She looked almost frightened. Nervous, he almost lost his resolve. "Say the word, Elizabeth, and I will stop this."

"No," she said with sudden sternness. "You must not stop!"

He smiled in relief and brought her hands to his lips. "Elizabeth Bennet, if you can love a man as foolish as I have been, I ask you, beg you, to consent to be my wife."

Elizabeth looked at him for several moments as though he had gone mad. "But, I——"

"I have been a fool—I am totally unworthy of your regard. But I *do* love you, Elizabeth. Can you manage to forgive me? Can you marry me?"

"How can this be? You said you could not," she sputtered, pulling her hands from his and hugging herself. She looked everywhere but at him. "You are bound by your responsibility to your family. You cannot ask me to permit you to dishonour that."

"My responsibility is to you, for it is you that I love, you who is the most worthy of my protection," he said, managing to capture her hands again. "I not only made a promise to you when we kissed, Elizabeth, I made a promise to your heart and mine. It is not something that can be discarded so carelessly. Love is a gift, and I promise to value yours for the rest of my life, if you will only allow it."

Elizabeth nodded slowly. It felt was as though she relied on his hands gripping hers to remain standing. Tears slid down her cheeks now, and his stomach burned with the fear she would refuse him.

Yes…yes," she said almost confused at first, then realization set in and she threw her arms around his neck. "Yes, yes, yes."

Relieved and overjoyed, Darcy pressed his nose in her hair and inhaled deeply. "Lizzy, Lizzy."

She pulled back and he kissed her thoroughly, tasting her lips, communicating his love for her in a way words never could.

"Do not go. My sister comes at the end of the week, and she will want to see you again. You all must stay at Pemberley," he said, one sentence rushing after another.

Elizabeth laughed aloud, and he saw the sparkle in her eyes that had been missing for much too long.

"I will go anywhere with you, Fitzwilliam," she whispered softly. He had never felt such joy in his life. Now, finally, he had done right. The answer had been there all along, waiting for him to accept its truth—love Elizabeth, be swept away...all would be well.

Chapter Twenty-five

Dearest Jane,

I am so happy I can scarcely write. So much has happened since I saw you last, for I have seen Mr Darcy again, and we are engaged! I am sure you had to read that sentence again. I almost cannot believe it myself. Everything has happened so fast, and the remainder of our travels have been foregone in favour of staying at Pemberley with Mr Darcy and his sister. The only person in the world I lack is you, dear Jane, and my merriment would be complete.

I expect to return to you for the second week in July, which is when Mr Darcy plans to visit my father. If all goes according to plan, we hope to be married by the end of August. I hope you will send us your congratulations. Who could have thought things would end in this happy way?

Send only my love to Charles, as Mr Darcy is writing his own letter to your husband, and one must expect he will express his own feelings in whatever way he finds most pleasing to himself.

I will see you soon, dearest Jane. Until then, you may spend all your time being deliriously happy for me.

Your Elizabeth

Elizabeth smiled as she set down her pen. She truly could never have imagined being such a happy creature. She turned her head and watched the man responsible for her present joy as he wrote his letters. In the moments after their engagement, Darcy had somehow managed to convince her uncle to stay with him at Pemberley, had ushered her back into the carriage, and had everyone travelling back toward the great house with him before Elizabeth had even regained presence of mind. Indeed, she had been in such a state of extreme relief and happiness that she had cared little what the plan for their destination had been.

She had yet to comprehend just what had affected the change in Mr Darcy to send him after them, but she would be forever grateful it had happened. They had agreed that after their letter writing, they would take a walk. Miss Darcy had arrived that afternoon, and most of the day had been spent supplying an explanation of all that happened in the short time between Darcy's arrival and her own. Miss Darcy had expressed her pleasure with the news most vehemently and had hugged both her brother and her new sister, discarding her usual shyness to welcome Elizabeth into the family. Now, after an eventful day, Elizabeth looked forward to some time alone with her fiancé.

"Miss Bingley is incorrect," she said to him as he carefully wrote his letter.

"Is she? How so?"

"You *do* write terribly slow."

"Yes," he laughed softly, "I do. Shall I abandon it until later?"

"I would not disrupt your thoughts."

"I believe you just have," he said, turning to smile at her. "I can come back to this."

Elizabeth rose, and they departed the house, headed out on their planned walk. She followed his lead, as he had expressed a wish to show her his favourite spot on the grounds. She wondered to herself how it was possible to have a favourite in such an array of beauty, but she discovered why he loved it so at once, when she saw he had led her to a small cluster of Linden trees, sunshine raining in amid the shade.

"Fitzwilliam, this is beautiful," she whispered, holding her hands palm up to catch the rays.

"My mother often came here to read. I would sometimes join her, and even after she was gone, I came. My father had that bench installed for her comfort."

Elizabeth spotted the seat he referenced and seated herself there. "I think I like this bench much better than those of my past."

Darcy's face tensed. "Yes." He came to sit beside her. "I have not made things easy for us."

"Fitzwilliam, if I may, I would ask what changed your mind."

She watched him exhale heavily but could not regret her question. Before she could truly accept that things were going to be different, she needed to hear him say why they had changed.

"It is times like these that a person wishes that there had been some fantastic reason, be it spells or mythical creatures, that impacted the foolish thinking and the ill-fated decisions they have made. I have no such excuse, Elizabeth. I am no epic hero; I am only a man. A man, that in his desperation to do what was right, chose wrongly. The greatest tragedy of all, however, was that I was not the only one to suffer the consequences—you have no idea how keenly I feel what I have done to you. I will never think back on my actions without pain."

Elizabeth placed her hand in his, and he clutched it tightly.

"I tried to go on, as I meant to, and do everything in my power to mend what had been damaged by my cousin's marriage. Every woman I met only spoke testament to fact that there is none your equal. I could not abide them, or anything it seemed, after our conversation. I was lost—I have been lost since long before I met you, and then——"

"Then we were lost again," she quietly finished for him.

"Two months ago, I visited my cousin and was witness to the happiest marriage I have ever seen. I did not quite understand it at the time, but it changed everything, Elizabeth. It made me think on things in ways I had never allowed myself before—how he was happy while I suffered; how that could be so when I was supposed to be the man that had done right.

"My cousin could not have known my feelings for you, or that I was attached to any woman, but he spoke to me in such a way that brought all that I had been through into question. He said he had learned that he had fallen in love with his wife not in spite of what she was, but because of it. I thought he must have been mad when he spoke so."

Elizabeth gave him a small smile. She could only imagine his reaction to such information.

"But it made me think and question myself, which was frightening to me, because I thought it my goal to have put it all behind me. I never could, but the conversation made everything fresh again—it was painful, but I was beckoned to be honest with myself.

"When I returned, I spoke to my sister, and the more time that passed, the more I agonized over it. I kept this by my side always." He pulled out the handkerchief he had carried as his constant companion and placed it in her hands. "It was a foolish thing, but this was the handkerchief I used to dry your tears that dreadful day in January. It came to represent all I had lost when I turned you away. Perhaps, now that we are happy, we ought to burn it."

"No," Elizabeth said clutching it protectively and bringing it to her nose. "It smells like you."

Darcy shrugged. "Well—"

"If you no longer care for it, I will keep it, for it means too much to throw away."

"If you wish."

"Finish your story, Fitzwilliam."

"When I saw you here at Pemberley, everything became clear, and I could not deny the truth anymore. In all honesty, I could not but expect you would refuse me without question, but I had to know. If there was the slightest chance you still felt for me as I did you, I had to ask you to marry me."

"I was never angry with you—I tried, but I was unsuccessful. I know my situation; I am not blind to the difference that lies between us. I could not fault your responsibility to your family. I punished myself for having loved you in the first place."

"I encouraged those feelings, Elizabeth. I will not allow you to defend me."

"I think, sir, if your suffering was in anyway similar to mine, there is no need for further punishment. I believe you are sincere. I love you too much to question your intentions beyond that."

"I do not deserve you," he whispered, brushing aside a lock of hair that fell in her eyes. They kissed tenderly, and Elizabeth leaned into the warmth of his kiss. His lips against hers, the taste of him was exquisite. His lips left hers when they both required air, and travelled from her chin to her neck. She sighed sweetly at the novelty of it. Elizabeth placed a palm on his cheek, and he pulled back to look at her.

"I could have lived without you, Fitzwilliam, but I would have never been whole. That is what your love is to me."

He turned his head and kissed her palm. "Oh, Lizzy, how did I ever think I could do without you?"

"You must know how relieved I am you found that you could not!" she laughed, happy tears beginning to prick at the corners of her eyes. "How I love you."

The skin on his shaven cheek was so soft and warm, and she had learned in the days since their engagement that she could not resist feeling it. His dark eyes were so expressive, they penetrated the very heart of her. She was indeed under his spell, and it was a great relief to know that she now had that right. While before she had loved with guilt, now there was nothing to come between them. Her happiness was unpolluted and genuine. She would never have to do without him again.

Chapter Twenty-seven

"Miss Bennet?"

Elizabeth opened her eyes and closed the book in her hands. Bleary-eyed, she looked around her and realized she must have fallen asleep in the library. Months of sleepless nights and the past week of over-excitement was beginning to catch up with her. She looked up to see Miss Darcy standing over her.

"Forgive me, I must have fallen asleep."

"I would not have woken you, Miss Bennet, but I believe my brother is looking for you."

Elizabeth smiled. In a house as large as this one, it was scarcely a wonder that more than one person was necessary to locate someone. They had been at Pemberley now for almost a fortnight, and the following week would see them parting ways again. It was no surprise that the couple were desirous of spending every available moment together.

"I will go and tell him I have found you," Georgiana said, leaving the room. Elizabeth watched her with interest. Georgiana Darcy was such a shy young lady that Elizabeth had been hard-pressed to find conversation with her. She could only hope that familiarity and time would make Georgiana easier in her presence. Before she could think further on the matter, however, Mr Darcy entered the room, a large smile on his face.

"I was beginning to think you were hiding from me."

"Never," Elizabeth laughed. "I had fallen asleep in here."

"There are rooms designed for that purpose, you know."

She smiled. Elizabeth loved when he teased her. Though it was very mild and infrequent, his humour was actually quite similar to her own.

"Your sister said you were in search of me. Was there something you required?"

"Nothing pressing. I only had something I wanted to ask of you."

"You may ask, sir, and I will decide if I wish to answer."

"How very gracious of you," he replied, rolling his eyes at her playful impertinence. "Too soon, we will have to part ways again for several weeks, and there will always be times when we must be apart."

Elizabeth nodded. She was no longer smiling.

"Though even the idea of being apart grieves me, I thought we might exchange a bit of ourselves for the other to keep with them when the original is not accessible to us." With that he opened his hand. In it, she recognized the miniature portrait of himself that Mrs Reynolds had shown them on their tour of Pemberley. Gingerly, she took it from his hands. She lightly ran her fingers over his likeness, then looked to the original with large eyes.

"I would be honoured to carry it with me, Fitzwilliam, but I have no such gift for you," she said sadly. "I have never sat for any portrait."

"I was sure that even if you *had* sat for a portrait, you certainly would not be carrying it with you," he replied.

"But, I have thought of something I would very much like to have if you would oblige me."

"Yes?"

"Lizzy—would you permit me…that is, I would very much like—"

He stopped himself in frustration and began anew. "If you would be so gracious as to allow it, Elizabeth, I had hoped you would donate a lock of hair for my keeping."

Elizabeth blushed, but her smile was in pleasure. It seemed very intimate to give him such a gift, yet she knew immediately she would gladly indulge him. Automatically, she removed the pins from her hair, and it fell about her shoulders. It was only seconds before his fingers were tangled in her curls.

"I assume you will know best how to acquire it," she said, turning to the side in an attempt to aid his progress. She closed her eyes as she felt his hands tenderly inspecting the ringlets for the one he wanted. When she heard the scissors snip, she felt a warmth in her belly that she could not explain. The delicacy of such an experience left her flushed and feeling very vulnerable to him. She turned to see him bring the ringlet to his nose to smell its fragrance.

"Lizzy, when you let down your hair, your scent filled my senses," he said, and she could see he was just as affected as she was by this intimate gesture. "You are beautiful."

She turned to him then and kissed him, placing her hands on his chest as his cradled her neck, holding her steady to receive his caressing lips against hers. The sweetness of his mouth left her breathless, and they were soon leaning on one another for support as they calmed and the kiss ended. Darcy buried his face in her hair, and she held him close for several minutes. It felt as though her skin was burning, and both were in awe of the intensity of feeling they had for one another.

In a week's time, their stay at Pemberley came to an end. She was to return to Yorkshire, he to Hertfordshire, seeking her father's consent. As the carriage pulled her away, Elizabeth clutched his portrait close to her heart, knowing that she had left a piece of herself with him, and rejoiced that neither of them would ever truly be alone again.

Chapter Twenty-Eight

It seemed to Elizabeth that Yorkshire had not varied from her initial assessment of it being the coldest place in the world. While her heart now rested warmly in her chest, the coolness in the air at Darnwell required extra care with her apparel and another blanket on her bed. Despite the chill, Elizabeth was very glad to see Jane again, and they spent no little time catching up. Although she had already related most of the particulars in her letter, Elizabeth shared again all that had precipitated what was now a very happy engagement between herself and Mr Darcy.

After a full week at Darnwell, Elizabeth sorely missed the presence of Mr Darcy from her life. They wrote every day, and as each new letter arrived, she could be seen hurrying down the path toward the sea to read his words in private. On one such day, Elizabeth received a rather thick missive directed from Hertfordshire. Knowing what information this particular letter likely contained, Elizabeth anxiously tore it open with trembling fingers. As she did, another letter fell into her lap.

Friday, 17 July 1812

Dearest Elizabeth,

I am pleased to announce that your father and I have spoken, and he has given us his blessing. I am now for London to make further arrangements, though in a week's time, I hope to be with you again.

As I am sure you will read in your father's message, he was not particularly grateful for our engagement. For myself, however, I can only bring myself to feel so much regret for his unhappiness, as by leaving Longbourn, you will become my very dear wife.

I hope this news is met with your pleasure, for I cannot express how relieved I am for your father's sanction of the

match. Until I see you again, my dearest Elizabeth, I shall
think and dream only of you.
With Love,
Fitzwilliam

Elizabeth smiled lovingly as she finished reading. Gently, she ran her fingertips against his signature, feeling the small indentions his pen had made. In a moment, she took up her father's letter. She was equally anxious to read his response, though Darcy had already indicated that their meeting had been a success. She was not surprised to find her father's letter to also be brief.

Thursday, 16 July 1812

Dear Lizzy,

*You may imagine my surprise when Mr Darcy arrived
this week to declare himself. While I might have been at
leisure to receive him thusly last autumn, I had quite
determined he was to join the ranks of young men
determined to cross my daughters in love.*

I listened to all he had to say, indeed I could see no way of avoiding it, and I gave him as much trouble as I could. In the end, I determined that I had better agree to this plan, if you are as adamant about it as your Mr Darcy.

He said he would wait for this letter from me before dispatching his own to you. I thought I had better get to it with some expedience, and after two days had passed, I knew it must be done immediately, and thus am writing this to you on the third day since our conversation.

I trust I have inconvenienced and pestered you both sufficiently enough for my own amusement.

Write soon, Lizzy, and tell me that this is all a misunderstanding and you will be home to stay.

T. Bennet

Elizabeth shook her head, smiling at her father's insufferable sense of humour. She had suspected he would take delight in teasing Mr Darcy to the extent of his tolerance. Indeed, Mr Darcy was certainly the very type of character her father routinely enjoyed pestering. He was oft solemn, very serious, and most of his interactions were conducted in a very businesslike manner. Naturally, her father would playfully interfere with Darcy's plans. When the opportunity presented

216

itself so conveniently, far be it from Mr Bennet's abilities not to indulge.

On the walk home, Elizabeth meditated on the misfortune that a full week and a half lay ahead before Darcy would join them. It seemed very hard to have to wait even a day longer to see him again. She removed the miniature that she kept constantly on her person and ran her finger over his dear face.

In spite of her relief to have acquired her father's blessing, a niggling thought continued to intrude upon her cheerfulness. Though everyone had expressed their happiness for their engagement, Elizabeth had noted that Jane had been rather restrained in expressing her congratulations. It concerned Elizabeth that her sister might yet harbour misgivings or ill-will toward Darcy. She hoped the passing days might do something to smooth such discontent over—she did not think she could bear it if her dearest sister and the man she loved could not be friends.

217

The sun was still high in the sky when Mr Darcy was spotted riding up to Darnwell house. Jane thanked the housekeeper, Mrs Edwards, for informing her of the arrival and immediately prepared herself to receive him. It was very unlucky that Mr Bingley had gone down to the docks, as well as Elizabeth having left for her usual afternoon walk. Jane had not expected to be required to greet Mr Darcy on her own. In spite of her sister's present happiness, Jane still felt a bit of frustration with this man who had caused them all so much grief and trouble. Regardless of how she had tried to forget it, the memory of Elizabeth's previous desolation prevented Jane from releasing her long-standing dislike. It seemed to her that he was the sort of man who chose to have only the things that were pleasing to him—hang everyone else. And now, because the very spoilt Mr Darcy had determined Elizabeth worthy of him, her sister could at last be happy. Compared to what her poor sister had suffered, things seemed to have worked out very conveniently for Mr Darcy. Nevertheless, Jane had not been so unkind as to mention these feelings to her husband or sister. Esteeming him as they did, it would have only caused them pain.

"Mr Darcy for you, Mrs Bingley."

Resolutely, Jane rose from her seat and greeted him with her usual kindness. She noted his distraction and determined he was looking for her sister.

"You find me quite alone this afternoon, sir. My husband and sister are usually not to be found before dinnertime."

Darcy nodded, and affected a smile. "Allow me to take the opportunity to thank you, madam, for your hospitality. You have a very lovely home here."

"Charles will be very glad to hear you say so. He has looked forward to having you stay with us almost as soon as we were settled. He greatly values your opinion, I think."

Jane searched his face for any indication of remorse and had only detected a twinge of guilt before Darcy replied, "I am sorry to have been required to stay away for so long. I assure you it stemmed more from necessity than from my own wishes."

"I am sure you came as soon as you could, Mr Darcy," Jane replied serenely. "I believe I owe considerable congratulations on your engagement to my sister. Lizzy informed us that you had successfully gained my father's blessing."

Darcy dipped his chin graciously and gave her an almost imperceptible smile. "I am a very lucky man, Mrs Bingley."

"Indeed," Jane said a little more tersely that she would have liked. Not surprisingly, Darcy picked up on her tone. The two eyed one another carefully.

"I would have been very astonished had you not looked on me with something like anger and distrust, Mrs Bingley."

Jane looked down at the hands clasped firmly in her lap. "I am only glad that my sister has found the happiness that she deserves."

"It would be inhuman for you not to consider me a villain, Mrs Bingley. G-d knows, I have often thought of myself in those terms this year." Darcy rose and came to stand before Jane.

"Truly, Mr Darcy, you owe me no such explanation."

"Yes, madam, I do," Darcy sighed, clasping his hands behind his back. "I have caused your sister, and no doubt yourself, quite a bit of pain and confusion. There is no question, I do not deserve Elizabeth, but I *do* love her—very much. I have not earned the happiness I currently enjoy, but I intend to spend the rest of our lives making amends to your sister. I was mistaken to deny her the place in my life that was rightfully her own. I cannot take back my actions, but I intend to learn from them as best I can. Elizabeth will never suffer from my hands again if it is within my power to prevent it. I hope, in time, for her sake, you might come to trust that I will never hurt her again— even if you find you cannot forgive me."

"Mr Darcy, you are the dearest friend of my husband, and are soon to be my brother. You have spoken plainly, and so will I. You will have my forgiveness," Jane said gently, then quietly added, "but know this— once you are irrevocably tied to us, you may be sure that I will exact appropriate revenge at my leisure if you disappoint me."

221

Darcy eyed Jane seriously for several moments. Jane squared her shoulders and glared back at him. She was not afraid of him and intended for him to know it. Suddenly, Jane perceived the beginnings of a smile from her opponent. Then, the most astonishing thing of all happened—he began to laugh. It was barely a chuckle at first, but as she began to laugh as well, it grew into generous guffaws from them both.

"Madam, do not think for a moment I take your warning lightly. I would not dream of inspiring your ire," he replied, and though he was smiling, Jane was able to determine he was serious.

It was into this scene of calming laughter that Elizabeth returned from her walk. Jane saw that the couple greeted one another with the utmost propriety, but noted that her own presence in the room was now painfully obvious to them all. She deliberated for only a moment, looking from one lover to the other, before determining to be merciful. She put her hand on Elizabeth's affectionately, then excused herself to speak with Mrs Edwards. Before she left, she pointedly assured them she would only be ten minutes.

As soon as Jane departed, Elizabeth left her seat and stepped into Darcy's embrace.

"You were earlier than you predicted," she whispered.

"I should have been back sooner had I known."

"I am afraid I was too impatient for the carriage and rode ahead."

"As usual."

"Yes," he smiled, and giving her a small kiss, he allowed just the tips of his fingertips to graze her neck. She shivered.

"Enjoy it now, sir," she advised, inclining her cheek to rest in the palm of his hand, "for once you are married, your wife will insist you remain in the carriage with her, impatience notwithstanding."

"When I am married, Lizzy, I shall have all that I want at my fingertips." He ran his free hand down her back in illustration of that fact. "I will have no need to rush."

"Mmm, a very pretty speech, Mr Darcy, but I suspect you will think differently when the time comes to make good on your promise."

223

Darcy watched her face for a moment, his smile slipping into a more thoughtful expression. He rubbed noses with her, and rested his forehead against hers. "Lizzy, I love you."

Elizabeth rose up on her toes and gave him a tender kiss, and in the heat of which, she expressed all the love she felt for him that there were no words to convey. He returned the kiss in kind, and they might have easily let themselves be carried away by such an action, but the awareness that Jane was due back at any moment induced them to soon pull back and compose themselves. However, Elizabeth made no move to return to her previous seat, preferring to remain beside Darcy. As promised, Jane returned promptly thereafter, and further intimacies were cast aside for more appropriate conversation.

Darcy excused himself when his luggage arrived, as he was desirous of a bath and a few moments' rest before Bingley returned. There was no doubt in Darcy's mind that his friend would be anxious to take him on a tour of the estate. Truthfully, he wanted nothing but to be alone with Elizabeth. Unfortunately, it was not to be, and he owed his friend more than that. He and Elizabeth were obliged to observe propriety for a month longer.

Despite weathering the man's teasing, Darcy had been pleased that his meeting had gone relatively well with Mr Bennet, and that he had not insisted upon a long engagement. While his betrothal to Elizabeth had its advantages, Darcy would not imagine enduring the dictates of proper behaviour for any great length of time. As it was, he found it becoming increasingly difficult to remain a gentleman in her company.

When it was ready, Darcy sank into the hot bathwater gratefully, washing away the dirt from the road as well as the kinks in his muscles. Although it had been somewhat uncomfortable, Darcy was thankful for his conversation with Jane. The lady had more than enough reason to feel sceptical of his feelings for her sister. He was determined to earn back the trust that had been lost with his previous actions—for Elizabeth's sake, he felt obligated to prove to those who were yet unconvinced how invaluable she was to him.

Chapter Twenty-nine

"Fitzwilliam?"

Darcy turned to the lady on his arm curiously. He and Elizabeth were taking one of their frequent walks. It had been found to be a very useful exercise for them to escape the house and the watchful eyes of Mr and Mrs Bingley.

"Do you believe Charles would permit you to escort me for a late evening walk?"

"How late are you suggesting?"

"Only as the sun is setting, out by the sea."

"If you wish it, I will ask him. I do not think he will be difficult to convince."

"If not, we shall have to sneak away," Elizabeth said seriously.

"I believe we would be very easily missed at that time of day, my love," he joked.

"Then you must gain his approval," Elizabeth advised.

As promised, Darcy sought Bingley out at the next opportunity. He was surprised to find his friend so reluctant to allow Elizabeth out at that time of night. Darcy had almost decided not to ask his reasoning when Bingley offered the information on his own.

"Darcy, you realize it is not safe to be walking out at night—for anybody. The last time Elizabeth was out of doors at night, she took ill. Did she happen to mention it?"

"When was Elizabeth ill?" Darcy asked, frowning deeply. The information hit his stomach like a brick.

"Toward the end of March. She had taken off earlier in the day and been gone much longer than anyone realized. When she was not present for dinner and could not be found in her rooms, we organised a search for her. I found her eventually, near the sea—she was wet-through from the rain. I have never seen a sight that frightened me more than her appearance then. She stared blankly out at the water, and due to the cold, she

227

looked almost ghostly. I bundled her as best as I could, but not surprisingly, she took a fever that evening. The whole experience terrified my poor wife dreadfully. Elizabeth recovered soon enough, but it was one of many such mishaps that came to be last winter."

A completely new kind of guilt came over Darcy as he leaned to rest his elbows on his knees. Why would Elizabeth wish to take him back there? Whatever it was, he believed it must be connected with that experience. "Elizabeth has not spoken much on what came to pass after we parted in London."

Bingley smiled mirthlessly. The wan expression did not suit his happy disposition. "Yes, well, perhaps that is for the best—it was a very worrisome time for Jane."

Darcy nodded but said nothing as his mind reeled over such information. He had known Elizabeth had suffered in those dark months, but to hear it in detail was another thing altogether.

"Bingley, I believe after hearing this story, there must be some significance to her wishing to show me. I can well comprehend your reluctance to allow it, but I assure you I would let no harm come to her from the expedition."

Bingley nodded quietly. "Jane will not thank me for permitting it, but I will do so. I trust your judgment acutely. I will only ask you to remember not to be out so long that you cannot find your way back should the lantern burn out."

و ﻝ و

"There it is," Elizabeth whispered. "Twilight."

Darcy took in the beautiful sight of the sun sinking into the ocean as darkness fell around them.

"Lovely," he said just as softly. They were seated together on the beach, Elizabeth leaning back into his embrace as the lulling sound of ocean waves crashing ashore enveloped them. Darcy affectionately rested his chin on her shoulder.

"I would come here whenever I could and watch the sky and the sea come together as one, if only for a little while, and close the abyss between them. It made me think of us and of how we had closed our own abyss for a time when we fell in love."

229

Darcy tightened his arms around her and placed a lingering kiss just beneath her ear. "What you have suffered, Lizzy."

"No, Fitzwilliam, no more of that. I brought you here to show you that we *are* this beautiful twilight. Our love is like twilight of the abyss—only now, we know that ours goes on and on. We shall live in twilight forever."

The overwhelming emotion Darcy felt from her speech made it impossible for him to speak. He turned her to face him and kissed her passionately. Elizabeth had shown a connection to his soul that irrevocably tethered his heart to hers. It was then that Darcy willingly gave himself over to Elizabeth for safekeeping. He belonged to her, and for all his supposed superiority and respectability, with her he was simply a man, completely swept away in the comforting arms of a woman's love. It was not a choice, it was a fact.

Elizabeth eventually pulled back and searched his eyes. Cognizant of the danger to overstepping decency, Darcy brushed back the curls that hung near her face. "Lizzy, I believe we had better go in."

"Just a few minutes more," she beseeched him. "I am not ready to return you to the dictates of restraint."

He kissed her again, relishing the weight of her against him, the feel of her in his arms. It was heartening to know that this was soon to be their forever. Elizabeth's breath tickled his senses as she trailed kisses along his jaw-line. It was at once unbearable and exquisite to feel her lips so lightly against his skin, and he involuntarily tightened his posture to brace himself. "Lizzy, can you know what you do to me?" he whispered desperately.

Her response was a soft laugh, and she ceased her assault by resting her head on his chest. He released the breath he was holding and soon relaxed in the warmth of her arms wrapped around him. Gently, he twirled one of her ringlets around his finger. *Lizzy*, he thought to himself. It was more than just a name to him. The word had become synonymous with comfort, safety, and love. Lizzy meant he had everything he needed. In a little while, they reluctantly left their spot on the beach and walked hand in hand toward the house. He kissed her one last time under the ebony cloak of night before they went inside and resumed the distance that was unpleasantly proper.

Chapter Thirty

All too soon, it was again time for them both to leave Darnwell. Elizabeth was to return to Longbourn and Darcy to London. It was a dreaded time that was forgivable only because it marked just two weeks until their wedding day. They parted with the promise to resume their daily writing. Darcy would return with Georgiana and his Fitzwilliam cousins in a week's time. Meanwhile, Elizabeth would submit to her mother's all and sundry wedding preparations.

Elizabeth went to her father as soon as she could, anxious to confirm that he had indeed bestowed his blessing in genuine. Though she was sure her father would never falsely give his approval, she was desirous to make certain he was not too unhappy with the plan. She found him in his usual repose, book in hand and a glass of port on the table beside him. Elizabeth instinctively curled up in the chair to his left, an action she had habitually taken since childhood. She flipped through another book that had been taken from the shelf while she waited for him to finish his chapter.

"It is a great pleasure to see you back in your usual place, Lizzy. Longbourn has not been the same since you went away."

"I have missed you too, Papa," she said, returning the book where she had found it. She smiled warmly at him.

"And yet, your young man informs me he intends to take you away forever. 'Tis very ungenerous of him."

"You are not *very* unhappy with my news, are you?" Elizabeth asked gently.

"Oh, I shall survive, if that is your meaning," he replied with a chuckle. "Though if I had known he wanted one of my daughters, I would have directed him toward Kitty or Mary to begin with."

Elizabeth laughed. "Not Lydia?"

"Oh, I am saving her for a very special kind of gentleman. I intend to amuse myself excessively in finding her a husband."

They both enjoyed a knowing laugh. "Papa."

"Yes, well," he murmured, watching her carefully. "You are a rare woman, Elizabeth. I should have known your intelligence would soon be appreciated by more than myself."

"Mr Darcy is the best of men, Father. I know I shall be very happy and cared for all the days of my life."

"Yes, yes, I suppose you shall, and better than I ever could have," Mr Bennet smiled. "I hope you will not forget us when you are Mrs Darcy."

"Never, Papa, you know that would impossible."

"I am sure your mother will now take delight in reminding you and everyone else that you are her child."

Elizabeth rolled her eyes with a smirk.

"A pity you and Jane were not my youngest. I would have had the pleasure of making you both take your time."

Elizabeth remained there with her father for some time, enjoying their usual comfortable silence. Truth be known, she had always relished being the one child always welcome in her father's study, while it was off-limits to the others. She knew she ought not take pleasure at being favoured, yet she had always been too happy to be in his company to regret his preference.

Mr Bennet was an enigma even to her at times. She did not understand many of his choices or actions, but as he had always turned a kind eye on herself, she had never thought to question him too deliberately. Even so, she was thankful that her own husband would not be so confusing and mysterious as her mother's. Darcy always told her his thoughts, as best he could, though one could discern it was not something he had made a habit of doing in the past. The fact that he was making an effort to do so for her was endearing. Fleetingly, she considered the general unfairness that some found such love while others did not, but predisposed to happiness as she was, it only worried her for a moment. Indeed, the thought of some of her acquaintance, namely her mother or Mrs Philips, being violently in love with *anyone* seemed impossible. Perhaps the love she felt for Darcy was meant for those who felt deeply—with very good luck.

Monday, 24 August 1812

Dearest Elizabeth,

I confess my stay in Town has not been a pleasant one. Do not trouble yourself. Georgiana and I are very well— only anxious to again be in your company. I have acquired the marriage license and will bring the settlement papers for your father as soon as I am able.

I have heard from my cousins. Colonel Fitzwilliam is already in Town, and has agreed to stand up with me on the blessed day. My other cousins, the viscount and his wife, are expected to arrive any day. On the following one, we intend to all make for Hertfordshire as a procession.

Thank your mother for offering to accommodate us, but we shall have to decline. I believe a party of five and servants would undoubtedly disturb Longbourn too inconveniently. Rosemont, luckily, has a friend who possesses a small getaway estate not far from Meryton, and he has generously offered to make it available for our use.

Georgiana has encouraged me to write how happy she will be to see you again. My own feelings I am sure you well know, yet I feel I must express them again. Never mistake that I think you the dearest creature in the world, and my heart shall ache for you until the happy moment when I will see you again.

With all my love,

F. D.

Elizabeth sighed as she closed his letter. In truth, she was actually enjoying her time at home. The months away had made the little town of Meryton somehow more endearing. Most of the people there she had known all of her life, and she enjoyed being amongst their simplicity again. As she knew this was the last bit of time she had as Miss Elizabeth Bennet of Longbourn, she had resolved to relish the opportunity of saying a proper goodbye to her childhood home, no matter how terribly she missed Darcy.

Elizabeth had learned that the best time to write to her fiancé was early morning, before her mother and sisters came downstairs. At that time of day, the house was very quiet, and lacked the pester of little sisters, stretching their necks to see what she was writing to Mr Darcy.

Tuesday, 25 August 1812

Fitzwilliam,

I will not ask questions of your postponing an explanation of why your time in Town has not been pleasant. I trust you will speak of it when we meet again. My mother will be disappointed that you will not stay at Longbourn, and thus, I ask you to prepare yourself for her reaction to the news. For my part, I see the merit in your party staying elsewhere. Longbourn has the tendency of feeling over-crowded as it is, and I would be truly sorry to scandalise your relations!

In contrast, my time in Hertfordshire has been enjoyable. It has been very good to meet with old friends again. Jane and Bingley have written that we may expect them on Monday. Mama has expressed her displeasure that they plan to be coming and going so briefly, but Jane had written that they intend to travel southward after the wedding. I think it a very good idea, as they have scarcely taken time to celebrate their own marriage.

I am very glad to know Colonel Fitzwilliam has agreed to stand up with you. I look forward to meeting him and your other cousins when you arrive. Please tell Georgiana that I have missed her, too, and look forward to seeing her again. As you might have expected, my mother has been very meticulous with every detail for our wedding, and while we have enjoyed several dinners and dances in the neighbourhood, the rest of my time is now spent confined to the house and helping her with planning. However, I must say that despite popular belief, I am certainly not as useful a bride as other ladies, and I suspect my poor mother would get on much better if she did not seek my assistance.

Nevertheless, I am certain that our wedding shall rival the splendour of Jane's as, my mother tells me, is only right. I do confess, however, that it would have been more convenient for me had you been a member of the clergy, as my mother restrained herself considerably for Mary's wedding to Mr Collins.

Come soon, Fitzwilliam, for I am sure my mother has many ideas to abuse you with before the happy day, Thursday next, as do I. You are sorely missed, and I long to have you with me again.

With love,

Your (very impertinent) Elizabeth

Chapter Thirty-one

Darcy's shoulders heaved with the residual anger that remained from the afternoon. He had known when he determined to marry Elizabeth that all of the internal conflict he had overcome would again be manifested through his uncle, Lord Desham. Indeed, the anger that pressed against his breast burned white-hot at the memory of his uncle's thoughtless words. He closed his eyes against the recollection, yet it was not an interaction he would soon forget.

"Out of all the insipid, ill-judged, and humiliating things you could have done, Darcy, I believe this is certainly the most ridiculous! I had thought better of you than to throw everything away on a useless country miss! Of all people to be taken in by a fortune hunter! George Darcy's son, no less."

242

Darcy had stood silent, his own expression conveying the fury he felt.

"Thoughtless! From *you*, of whom we expected everything! You could have had any number of suitable ladies, even your cousin, Anne, would have been appropriate, if you did not care for the business of choosing a wife. Darcy, I demand you abandon this genuinely absurd notion at once!"

"I am only determined to promote my own happiness, and that of the woman I love," Darcy replied quietly. "I was not at all inconvenienced with the responsibility of choosing a wife, and chose a lady I held in high esteem and affection."

"The woman you love!" the earl mimicked hotly. "Darcy, the woman you love has looped you, no doubt by disgracing herself, into a marriage that must be impossible. This is a match based upon deceit and artful behaviour, and I will not stand by and allow you to make yourself a fool. You dishonour us all to promote your contemptible happiness! How could you ever be happy knowing what you have done to us?"

"I have done nothing to *you*, sir. It is you who is determined to connect yourself in my affairs."

"As head of this family, I am inextricably connected with *all* of your affairs!" Lord Desham roared. "You will abandon this plan."

"I will not."

"And so you are determined to see the further ruination of our name? A name built upon generations of respectability and pride? You will make yourself and your wife ridiculous in the way my son has done. Would you have the world speak of this woman as they have Gregory's?"

Darcy said nothing, the tightening of his jaw the only indication he had heard.

"You have a responsibility to this family! You must think sensibly lest we be forced to turn our backs on you."

Darcy shook his head. "You will do no such thing."

"Do not test my resolve, Darcy, you will be sorely disappointed."

"What of Georgiana? You turn from me, and she will suffer for it."

The earl ignored Darcy's point, signifying its truth. Yet he persisted. "I cannot disown my son, Darcy, but for *you* I have no such obligation."

"I beg your pardon, sir, but you imply that it is within your power to disown me. That would be impossible, sir, for I am beholden to no man, and I am not yours to dismiss as you please. While I respect your feelings and feel the honour of our connection, I am not your son, and my respectability—everything that is mine—is no one's for the giving or taking. At the death of my father, I became my own man with a man's responsibilities, and I will answer to no person for my actions. I am thankful for our connection, sir, and I hold your authority in great esteem. However, where that ends is when you attempt to impose yourself on my private matters. I will not heed the demands of a man who asks me to cast aside the woman meant by G-d to be my wife. I will not permit you to come into my home and address me as you would an ignorant child. You will respect the wife of my choosing, or you will no longer be welcome in my home or the lives of the people who reside there. Have I made myself clear?"

"And this is how you speak to your elders? To your mother's brother, no less!" the earl exclaimed, his eyes wide with outrage.

"It is how I will address any person who enters my home and dares to question my judgment, who insults my fiancée with the intent of disrespecting me in every possible way."

Uncle and nephew glared at one another silently for several moments, neither willing to abandon their position. Any person who happened to see them in those moments would have remarked on how clearly they favoured. The same dark expression, the same square jaw set in stubborn fury, both feeling themselves to be completely in the right. It was Darcy that spoke first.

"If you have nothing further to say to me, I must ask you to leave, for on this subject, I do not intend to yield."

Lord Desham seethed in anger as he turned to leave. "May I be thankful your father is dead, that he be spared of knowing what his son has become."

Darcy started visibly at such a cruel sentiment. His eyes flared with barely tethered rage.

"Be gone!" he boomed.

"It is my wish that we never meet again."

"On something, at least, we are in perfect agreement," Darcy had replied evenly.

In the hours that had passed since the interaction, Darcy had remained as incensed as he had been watching Lord Desham turn his back and angrily leave the room. He had suspected the earl would not be pleased with his decision, but he had not expected such angry and hateful words to pass between them. Nevertheless, Darcy did not regret the things he had said or his decision to marry Elizabeth. Nothing in his life could promise him a happiness that rivalled what he felt for her. If it required estrangement from his uncle, so be it. They had never been particularly close in any case—none of his relations had been there in those dark hours after his father's death and in the subsequent months as he struggled to take over and preserve all that Mr Darcy, Sr. had left behind.

247

He had been alone then, save for his cousins and Georgiana, and he could no longer contemplate his uncle's interference in his personal life. Desham had never shown him consideration when he needed it most, and Darcy was not willing to accept it now. It had been a very long time since he had allowed himself to need anybody, and even so, never so much as he knew he needed Elizabeth. He would not allow others to stand in the way of his happiness ever again. He had played by the rules and lost. Life from this point would be on his own terms, and he would not apologise to anyone for the choices he had made. He would choose happiness, and he would choose Elizabeth.

Chapter Thirty-two

"Lizzy, sit down!" Lydia complained. "You are standing in my light!"

Elizabeth looked back at her sister apologetically, seeing Lydia was redecorating a bonnet. In truth, she owned her restlessness must have been distracting. She expected Darcy to arrive every moment, and had difficulty remaining still. She rolled her eyes at her behaviour. To have to be scolded to her senses by *Lydia* of all people! She sat down and picked up her book. She had been on the same page all morning. She simply could not make herself concentrate on the words. All she could think of was Darcy and how she would see him that day. She felt very silly, but there it was.

Darcy cursed as the carriage rattled over another pothole. He looked up to see his sister watching him curiously. He blushed at using such language in front of her.

"Forgive me," he sighed.

"You are in quite a temper today."

"I am only anxious for this trip to be over."

"And to see Miss Bennet," Georgiana supplied smugly.

Darcy turned his head to gaze out the window.

"Do not worry, Brother, I am sure she waits longingly for you in Hertfordshire."

Darcy glared at her, and she laughed.

"The carriage ride is hurting my back," he complained petulantly.

"You always say so, and then you take off on your horse the first chance you get," Georgiana replied, letting him know he was not so mysterious as he thought.

He glanced at Mrs Annesley, only to see her looking serenely out the window. He rolled his eyes and huffed again.

Ten minutes of book reading had still not found Elizabeth on a new page. Finally, she gave in and resolved to take a walk. She supposed that as long as she remained near the house, she would know when the Darcys arrived. As soon as she was outdoors, she broke into a run down the hill in an attempt to give relief to the nervous energy she felt. When she got to the bottom, she laughed and spun around and around childishly.

It was a beautiful autumn day, the sun was shining, the air was beginning to crisp and Elizabeth felt all the relief being out of doors can bring. The four walls of Longbourn had done little to ease her anxiety, but in the fresh air, she felt less constricted. After the previous autumn, there was no way that particular field could escape her memories of Darcy. How many times had they walked this way together during his stay at Netherfield? So much had passed since then, it seemed so long ago, and yet just like yesterday.

"Lizzy!"

Elizabeth turned her head at the familiar voice. "Charlotte!" she cried, and they embraced laughing.

"It has been so long since I have seen you, I wondered if it truly was you there. But then I heard your laughter and knew it was you."

"It seems so long since we have walked this way together."

"I do not know if I said so at the Heeleys' the other night, but I am truly happy for you, Lizzy," Charlotte said, linking arms with her.

"Thank you."

"The first time I saw you and Mr Darcy together, I knew how it would be."

"How can that be so?"

"He always displayed a particular regard for you."

"You mean he did not ignore me altogether," Elizabeth laughed.

"Yes," Charlotte smiled. "I suppose that was it. You will be very much missed in this part of the world, my friend."

Elizabeth leaned her head against Charlotte's shoulder.

"I hope we shall always be friends."

"Look, Lizzy, a carriage has pulled up."

"Oh!" Elizabeth cried, releasing Charlotte's arm and hurrying back up the hill.

For as long as he lived, Darcy would never forget the sight of Elizabeth spinning and laughing amongst a sea of dandelions. She looked so beautiful and carefree that had he not been so in love, he would have fallen again and again until there was nothing else. The carriage moved again from view of Longbourn, but Darcy remained mesmerized. His heart thundered impatiently in his chest for the few minutes left before their arrival. He was passively aware that Georgiana had said something, but he was lost to it, for up the hill Elizabeth came running, and he was out of the carriage to greet her. Mindlessly, he handed down his sister before turning back to Elizabeth and kissing her fingers. She stared up at him, smiling as she caught her breath.

Charlotte cleared her throat, and they both snapped out of their trance. Distractedly, Elizabeth turned her head as if noticing their friends for the first time. She stepped back and Darcy dropped her hands. Only then did he realize Miss Lucas was there.

"Forgive me," he said, recovering himself. "Miss Lucas, please allow me to introduce my sister, Georgiana."

"I am very pleased to meet you, Miss Darcy," Charlotte said, obviously amused by the display she had just witnessed.

At length, Charlotte excused herself, and Mr Darcy and his sister were escorted into Longbourn where Mrs Bennet greeted them with enthusiasm. Darcy looked over to discern his sister's reaction, noting surprise and fatigue. In his haste to see Elizabeth, he had thoughtlessly brought her along. Georgiana endured the conversation of Mrs Bennet and her daughters as best she could, though he saw she was exhausted. A glance confirmed she was intimidated by Elizabeth's mother. Nevertheless, he had come to see Elizabeth, and he could not bring himself to leave again without even a moment alone with her.

"Mrs Bennet, I wonder if I might have a private audience with Miss Bennet?" he asked only to see his little sister look over to him, eyes wide as saucers. "I will only be a moment and then we must be going."

"Of course!" Mrs Bennet exclaimed. "Lizzy, take him to the day room."

Obediently, Elizabeth rose from her chair and guided Darcy away from the others. As soon as the door was safely closed, Darcy pulled Elizabeth into his arms and kissed her, conveying how sorely she had been missed in the week away.

"We cannot stay long," he whispered. "Georgiana is very tired, but I could not depart without a moment with you. I am so glad to see you, Lizzy."

He relished the feel of her cheek pressed against his chest.

"I am glad you came, if only for a short time. I have had my eye on the road all afternoon watching for you."

He kissed her again, leaving them both flushed and breathless. They remained together in that way for several minutes, collecting themselves, and holding one another close.

"I love you, Lizzy," he said, smoothing the errant curl that had fallen upon her forehead. "And come Thursday, you will be my wife."

"Yes," she smiled at the thought. "It cannot come soon enough."

A few minutes later, the Darcys had gone, leaving Elizabeth standing in the doorway, her lips still tingling from his kisses.

Chapter Thirty-three

"Miss Bennet, Miss Catherine Bennet, and Miss Lydia Bennet for you, sir."

"Bring them in," Rosemont said with a smile. The whole party found themselves very cheerful that moment, as Colonel Fitzwilliam had just told them a very amusing story about a bumbling man unintentionally assaulting a shopkeeper.

Everyone rose to greet the Bennet sisters. Elizabeth's quick eyes took in all of their appearances. She saw a pleasant man and woman seated close together, both elegantly dressed, though not in an officious sort of way. The other gentleman then, could only be Colonel Fitzwilliam, though his uniform made that all the more obvious. She could discern by their genuine expressions that they were very pleasant people.

"Elizabeth, Miss Catherine, Miss Lydia, allow me to present my cousins, The Viscount and Lady Rosemont, and Colonel Fitzwilliam," Darcy spoke. When the initial pleasantries had been exchanged, they were all seated again, with Elizabeth and her sisters placed beside Mr Darcy. It took Elizabeth only a few moments to see that Lady Rosemont was both young and shy. That she would have such a formidable title was almost farcical, for this woman was no more commanding than Georgiana. Nevertheless, Kitty and Lydia sat in awe of her. Elizabeth felt the need to draw the lady out.

"And how do you like Hertfordshire, Lady Rosemont, does it suit well?

"Very well, Miss Bennet, I thank you," her voice was also very quiet and sweet.

"I am so pleased you will be with us for the wedding. I have met very few of Mr Darcy's relations."

Lady Rosemont blushed. "I am a very new relation myself, Miss Bennet. But Gregory was very glad to come as soon as Mr Darcy wrote to him."

Elizabeth smiled as Lady Rosemont placed her hand lightly on the viscount's forearm, and the couple shared a loving glance. Darcy had not exaggerated the couple's regard for one another. She felt Darcy's hand brush hers, and she smiled up at him. *Hello*, she mouthed, and he dipped his chin graciously with a small smile.

Too late, Elizabeth realized that Colonel Fitzwilliam had seated himself near Kitty and Lydia. Immediately, their quiet awe of Lady Rosemont transferred to noisy giggles and conversation with Colonel Fitzwilliam.

"I hope you do not plan to leave the neighbourhood after the wedding, Colonel, our hearts will be *broken*!" Lydia informed him. "Our friends will never believe we have sat with such a handsome colonel."

"Lydia," Elizabeth whispered in admonishment.

"Sir William will certainly host an assembly if he knew you all were here," Kitty added.

"You must dance with us all!" Lydia finished.

Elizabeth felt the mortified blush creep up her neck. In the months away from them, Elizabeth had quite forgotten the painful embarrassment her sisters could

259

evoke. She was surprised to hear the booming laughter that came from the viscount.

The gentleman elbowed his brother very hard as he said, "Well, we cannot permit the breaking of any hearts can we, Edward?"

The colonel turned his head, and Elizabeth perceived the wide smile he also wore. She exhaled as her ease was recovered.

"I daresay if there are assemblies and dancing while we are here, it would be beyond me to avoid it. I would quite like to become better acquainted with you all," the colonel replied genuinely.

Mindlessly, Elizabeth turned to Darcy to gauge his disapproval, but found him looking down at her, obviously more concerned with how she managed her sisters' behaviour than any other person.

"Miss Bennet?" came the soft voice of Lady Rosemont. "I wonder if you would take the air with me?"

Elizabeth smiled. "Of course," she grazed her hand lightly on Darcy's knee as she rose and followed the lady out of doors. They walked in silence for some time, and Elizabeth was just beginning to search for some sort of conversation when her companion spoke.

"Thank you for walking out with me, Miss Bennet."

Elizabeth gifted her with a smile. "I love walking. I was more than eager to accept your offer."

"I hope you will not think me presumptuous, Miss Bennet, but I did want to speak to you. You see, I am so glad to meet Gregory's relations, new and old."

"Yes," Elizabeth agreed encouragingly.

"You must not worry about your sisters' behaviour in his presence. Gregory is not like most men of his station. He sees such enthusiasm for what it is—the brightness of youth. He will not fault them for it."

Elizabeth raised her eyebrows. "That is very kind, however, his opinion is not a popular one in general."

Lady Rosemont seemed to fidget a bit. "I did not offend you?"

"No," Elizabeth chuckled. "It is no secret that my younger sisters can be a bit challenging."

"I did not mean to say—forgive me."

Elizabeth endeavoured to change the subject. "Mr Darcy tells me you are very lately married yourself."

"Yes, we have not been married a year."

"You both seem very happy."

"Yes," Lady Rosemont agreed softly. "We are very fortunate."

They walked in silence a while longer, as Elizabeth was at a loss for conversation, and none came from her companion.

"I do not suppose it is possible that you have not heard," Lady Rosemont said, breaking the silence at last. "You must know I am responsible for the upset in your fiancé's family."

Elizabeth did not know how to respond. She inclined her head in the affirmative but did not venture a reply.

"I never meant to cause so much trouble."

"Sometimes trouble is unavoidable."

Lady Rosemont smiled sadly. "I believe my husband to know his own mind well enough to make decisions that promote his own happiness. It was how I finally reconciled myself to accepting him. In the beginning, I refused him."

Elizabeth glanced at her companion in surprise.

"I knew the difference in our lives—what was meant for us in our respective stations. It was madness to think I would be accepted amiably as his wife. How could I willingly enter into an agreement that would only harm his reputation in the eyes of the world? It would have been the height of selfishness, I believed. I cried for two days after he left—I loved him with all my heart, Miss Bennet."

"But he came back to you?" Elizabeth encouraged, now fully interested.

"Yes, he came back. He said he would not accept my refusal, knowing as he did of my feelings for him. I do not know if I ought to regret my actions, but I chose to trust him.

"When you accepted Mr Darcy's proposal, he wrote to my husband, and thus I know all that you have overcome together. I have never felt such happiness in my life as I do with Gregory, and for that reason I cannot regret my choice. As long as my husband does not regret, I never will. I have said all of this to one end, Miss Bennet. I wanted you to know that I feel for the magnitude of your present happiness, and I know what apprehension you may be feeling to be joining a family who disapproves of you, though to a lesser degree, as you are a gentleman's daughter. I wanted to tell you that Gregory and I feel nothing but joy for your marriage, and that I hope…more particularly, that we might be friends."

At the end of the lady's speech, Elizabeth felt tears welling in her eyes, so touched was she at the gesture. "I would like that very much, Lady Rosemont. You cannot know how much you confiding in me has meant. I would be very honoured to call you my friend.

"Then please, you must call me Lillian."

"Only if you agree to call me Elizabeth."

With this new agreement, the ladies turned back to the house, chatting cheerfully about the upcoming wedding. Elizabeth felt all the significance of Lady Rosemont's point to make her acquaintance more particularly. She was both pleased and glad to have made such an unlikely friend. Come what may from their husbands' family, they each would now have an ally.

The moment they rejoined the others, Elizabeth locked eyes with Darcy. The warmth of his gaze made her stomach flutter. She seated herself beside him and inclined her head in his direction. Quietly, she related the reason for her excursion with Lady Rosemont.

"I had hoped to gain a few moments with you myself," he said where only she could hear.

Elizabeth smiled at the note of peevishness in his voice. "Perhaps you might suggest another excursion before we leave."

Darcy did not reply, and she knew her idea was likely too obvious. "Will you visit Longbourn tomorrow?"

He shook his head. "I will try, but tomorrow will be a very busy day for us both."

Elizabeth sighed. It seemed they would not gain another chance to speak alone before their wedding. "You might suggest we *all* walk out?"

He nodded gently, but did not look hopeful.

"My sisters did not embarrass themselves too severely in my absence, I hope."

"Miss Lydia might have embarrassed a lesser man, but Fitzwilliam is fortunate enough to possess a quick mind and easy conversation. I believe both of my cousins have opted to be amused by her remarks."

"Very generous of them," she whispered, eyeing her sisters warily.

"Where is your elder sister today? I had thought she would have been with you."

"She has gone into Meryton with my mother. An acquaintance of ours, Mrs Evans, has died. They have gone to pay their respects."

"Ah," he replied. "I am sorry to hear it."

"How does Georgiana fare?"

"She fares as best she can in this, as well as any conversation," he sighed. And they both looked to Georgiana just as she was looking over to them. Discreetly, she rose and sat next to her brother. Elizabeth could barely hear her voice as she spoke.

"Brother, I will suggest a walk, and you may invite Elizabeth."

Elizabeth glanced gratefully as Darcy's little sister. When Darcy agreed, she did just as she suggested, and soon the three of them set out on Elizabeth's second walk of the afternoon, Georgiana walking ahead.

"Your sister is very thoughtful."

"And I very thankful," Darcy laughed.

"In but two days, we will no longer require artfulness to be together."

"It cannot come quickly enough."

"No," Elizabeth agreed. Once Georgiana had turned a corner, Darcy led Elizabeth to the side of the house and claimed his first kiss of the day. Happily, she ran her fingers through his hair, resting them at the nape of his neck.

"Fitzwilliam, will you tell me why your trip to Town was so unpleasant?" she said when they had resumed their walk.

Darcy grimaced, and Elizabeth wondered if she might be better off not knowing. "My uncle and I quarrelled, as I had expected we would. He used every method available to persuade me to reconsider my engagement. His only success was to infuriate me without repair. We did not part on cordial or speaking terms. I have rarely been so angry in my life."

"Fitzwilliam, I never meant to create a breach within your family, I—"

"Elizabeth, it matters not, I want you to be my wife. I cannot do without you, such is my love. I will not permit any person in my life that refuses to give the proper respect that is due to you as my wife. You are my family, as are those who value happiness over the frivolities of wealth and social standing. Your place is with me, and if there are those who wish to deny that truth, they will find themselves very unwelcome in my life," he said with vehement determination. "I am not fool enough to make the same mistake twice."

Elizabeth did not reply, instead she clutched his arm all the more possessively as they walked. Eventually, she said gently, "I care for nothing if I may be with you. If you do not regret, neither shall I." She smiled at the sentiment so reminiscent of what Lady Rosemont had said of herself only an hour before.

Chapter Thirty-four

When the visit came to an end, the Bennet girls returned to Longbourn. As Darcy had predicted, the following day was a long one. As the addition of Jane and Bingley had added to the already chaotic scene, the house now buzzed with last minute preparations and emotions. In the afternoon, Elizabeth received a note from Darcy expressing his regrets at not being available to visit on this last day of their engagement.

In spite of her family's general silliness, Elizabeth chose to spend the day enjoying her final hours at home as Miss Bennet. Tomorrow, everything would change, and though she welcomed her marriage, she also knew it had truly been a favour to have grown up in such a noisy house with lots of noisy people. Longbourn had character, and the constant buzz of activity, friends, and laughter had shaped her into the happy, compassionate, and easy creature she was now. That evening, the Bennets all sat together at dinner, with only Mr Bingley in Mary's place creating variance to how they had passed dinner all of Elizabeth's life.

"Upon my word, I have never seen such a handsome corpse as Mrs Evans!" her mother related once they were all settled. Immediately Mr Bingley began coughing, and Elizabeth knew he had inhaled some of his soup. She bit her lips and took a sip of water.

"Is that so?" Mr Bennet smiled. "Excellent."

"Oh yes, indeed. I can only hope I am as favoured to be looking so well when I am dead," his wife replied.

Lydia snorted and rolled her eyes.

"I may be mistaken, my dear," Mr Bennet began, cutting his meat, "but I was not aware that the deceased cared for such finery."

"*Lord*, who cares what a person looks like when they are dead?" Lydia cried, obviously put-out by the topic.

"Your mother is determined to always look her best, Lydia. If someone were to dig her up, she would not want to alarm them with her appearance."

270

Jane and Elizabeth shared an amused look as Elizabeth stifled her laughter behind a napkin.

"You know, she did not look too young or too old, she looked exactly as she ought," Mrs Bennet continued, ignoring them.

Mr Bennet chuckled. "Mrs Evans was *just right* then, aye, Lizzy?"

Elizabeth lowered her napkin and cast her father an amused, but warning look.

"I shall never forget when Mrs Cox died, and they had her looking so very young. Why, she looked to be only thirty-five, though she was nearly twice that. Everyone went on and on with how well she looked. For my part, I think a person ought to be looking their own age when they are shown."

"I suppose you found Mrs Evans to be looking every day of her sixty years," Mr Bennet smiled.

"I should not care at all how I am looking when I am dead. I shall be *dead*!" Kitty insisted.

"Yes, you do, foolish girl! Would you have the whole neighbourhood speaking of how ill you looked?"

271

And thus began an argument where Kitty maintained she would not care, and Mrs Bennet insisted she would. It was only when they were leaving the table that the subject was abandoned.

Elizabeth went to bed that night, her head full of the past, present, and future. Her family at Longbourn would always be her family. They were silly and oft embarrassing, but they were all dear to her in their own ways. Now she had her wedding on the morrow, and it was time to say goodbye to them all and go away with her husband. She looked forward to it with all her heart, but it would be foolish to say she would not miss them.

Lydia and Kitty had insisted she stay with them that night, and so she found herself in between both of them on the bed, enduring their customary bickering and now their questioning her about how excited she must have been. It was late into the night when she got them to be silent, and even later before she closed her own eyes. A mixture of anticipation and nervousness swirled in her head. Tomorrow everything would change. The last thought she had before falling asleep was wondering if Darcy lay awake as she did, and wondering if his thoughts tended in the same direction. The thought of Darcy and his kisses calmed her, and soon she drifted off into a dreamless slumber, the moonlight in the window already casting radiance on the promise tomorrow would bring.

Chapter Thirty-five

Elizabeth smoothed her frock with shaking hands.

"Oh Lizzy, you are so beautiful," Jane breathed as she fussed with the already perfect arrangement of curls atop Elizabeth's head.

Elizabeth smiled but did not reply. She was exceedingly nervous, and her fingers continued to shake as she adjusted the neckline of her dress. The day was here at last, and it at once seemed very real, yet dreamlike. Countless times she had whispered in disbelief, "This is my wedding day." As she murmured it again, she felt her heart flutter. No, it would not be real until she saw Darcy. Lydia and Kitty came in then, both also expressing how beautiful she looked.

"Mr Darcy will be wild in love with you when she sees you," Kitty advised.

"He is already wild in love with her, Kitty," Lydia argued. "He looks at her as though his eyes will pop out of his head. They will have ten children before anyone knows it."

"Lydia!" Elizabeth and Jane admonished simultaneously.

"Oh well, never you mind," Lydia laughed. "I am sure you will be happy together, but you must promise to have him smile more, Lizzy!"

"Lydia, I have no such control over Mr Darcy's facial expressions," Elizabeth advised, gently placing her bonnet over her hair.

"Make haste, girls, it is almost time!" Mrs Bennet called from down the hall.

Elizabeth found her father waiting for them in the foyer. They stepped into a tight hug that conveyed to Elizabeth just how much love her father felt, giving her away this day. After a while, he offered her his arm, and she took it. There was a sad silence between them today, as each of their hearts was heavy at the prospect of parting. Next to Jane, her father would be the most difficult to leave behind.

In those last moments, she clutched his arm tightly, allowing him to be her protector for those remaining minutes. He looked down at her, and she smiled dearly at him. As they were poised to enter the church, she turned her face toward his ear and whispered, "There will always be a place in my heart that is yours alone, Papa."

His response was to take a deep breath and pat her hand affectionately. Together they faced Mr Darcy and the rector, who waited for them at the end of the aisle. It was at that moment that the acceptance of reality weighed upon her. When Mr Bennet placed her hand in Darcy's, a wave of elation washed over her, and she felt the significance of what was about to happen to her life. She looked into Darcy's eyes as tears slid down her cheeks.

The ceremony was quick but heartfelt, as nary a bride and groom spoke their vows so honestly as did Darcy and Elizabeth. When they were pronounced man and wife, a smile like she had never seen graced Darcy's already handsome features.

276

Today I am Mrs Darcy, she thought one last time as Darcy led her out of the church. She laughed brightly as the coins were thrown in the air around her.

The wedding breakfast had been lovely, though Darcy was sure he would not have noticed if it had been poorly done. The sort of joy he experienced, he reckoned, was the sort that only comes once in a lifetime. Now, riding in the carriage, he clutched Elizabeth's gloved hand tightly, kissing it another time with every minute that passed.

When he had seen her make her way down the aisle on the arm of her father, his breath had caught in his chest. He had never loved another person as he did Elizabeth, and felt all the solemnity necessary to earnestly accept her as his wife for now to all eternity. They had survived so much, inflicted upon them from the world, and some his own doing, but they had made it through those dark times. She had such a rosy blush on her cheeks as she smiled up to him just then. She had told him in a private moment that there was nothing she desired more than being his wife. His heart had grown three sizes since they had met, and she had taught him what it meant to love unconditionally.

He leaned down so his lips were near her ear and whispered, "You are unbelievably lovely today, my own."

She blushed deeper. "Thank you, Fitzwilliam. How can I express how happy I am to know I shall never have to do without you again?"

"I believe you just did," he laughed.

"Fitzwilliam."

"Mmm?"

"I am not afraid."

"Neither am I."

"Never again," she said as he pressed a gentle kiss to her lips. Soon though, their conversation lulled, and Elizabeth fell asleep against his shoulder.

At length, they came to a stop in front of the Darcy townhouse in London. Darcy nudged his new wife to wake and easily helped her down from the carriage. They sat through a simple dinner, and ended their evening by retiring almost abruptly afterward.

As Elizabeth waited for her husband to join her, she reflected upon all that had happened since she had first met Mr Darcy. In less than a year's time, the Bennets had married three of their five daughters, leaving only Kitty and Lydia at home. How many times had she thought herself destined to be the last sister at Longbourn? She had never allowed herself to hope that things would end in such a happy way.

She looked around her new accommodations and was astonished by its beauty. Her bedroom was adorned in cream and ivory coloured bedding. The walls themselves were decorated with the fine linings of flowered wallpaper. Beside the bed, there lay a table where Elizabeth had found a new mirror and hairbrush left as a wedding present from her husband. Everything in the room was new to her, and yet she embraced its cosiness as she settled herself amongst the bed-pillows.

"Lizzy?"

Elizabeth turned her head to see Darcy's dear face, watching her with trepidation. She smiled in a way she hoped would ease the nervousness he obviously felt. In invitation, she held her hands out, beckoning him to join her there. When they were settled in the plush blankets of her bed, Elizabeth curled next to him and rested her chin on his shoulder.

"I am so happy, Fitzwilliam."

"As am I," he said, running his fingers tenderly down her back.

Epilogue

"Mama! Papa! Look!" Claire Darcy cried as she ceased her running ahead and stopped to pick up a treasure she had found near the water.

"Claire, make sure that shell does not have any inhabitants before you pick it up," Darcy warned as he shifted his infant son's weight to his other arm. Little Gregory gurgled happily as his mother tickled his feet from beside them. Eventually, they caught up with Claire, who was collecting many a precious seashell in her skirts.

The Darcys had arrived at Darnwell only yesterday, a tradition they had kept every Easter since their marriage five years earlier. Since then, the Bingleys had added two very well-mannered children to their brood, and the Darcys were expecting their third. If it was warm enough, as it was this year, the entire family would traipse down to the beach to enjoy a picnic by the sea and this outing resulted in Claire's preoccupation with seashell collecting.

Elizabeth seated herself beside Jane on the blanket and opened her arms for little Charles to tumble into her lap. His cherubic blond hair and blue eyes had always served as a weakness for his Aunt Lizzy, who could never resist a cuddle from him. As Claire was making herself very messy with all the sand, Darcy handed Gregory to Jane and went to see to her.

With time, Jane had been able to abandon her own prejudices against her brother-in-law, and she had learned to look on him with respect, rather than distrust. Even she could not fault how fervently he loved Elizabeth, and it heartened her to know that her dear Lizzy had gotten her happy ending after all.

Lord and Lady Desham had never quite forgiven Darcy or their son for such imprudent marriages, but time and the desire to present a united front in society had beckoned them to accept what they could not change. Nevertheless, for Darcy, the relationship with his uncle would be forever strained by the terrible conversation that had preceded their estrangement.

As Lady Rosemont had hoped, she and Elizabeth had become the dearest of friends and had corresponded regularly over the years. Georgiana, who had yet to marry, was currently visiting with them for the holiday.

Elizabeth turned her head at the sound of her daughter's laughter and saw her husband holding Claire over the water to rinse her hands of sand.

"The sun is setting," Jane remarked, mildly. "We had better be going in."

"Yes," Elizabeth agreed, but made no move to do so. Over the years, she had never shaken her love of ocean twilights and watched mesmerized as the orange and pink sun melted into the water. In the background, she could hear the delighted laughter of Edward Bingley as his father chased him away from the water. In less than a few moments, Jane had managed to pack up their picnic and was calling at Edward and his father to tell them that she was going in with little Charles. As usual, the Darcys lagged behind, all holding hands as they

283

walked slowly back inside, Elizabeth and Darcy's eyes watching as the sky fell into twilight.

"It never loses its beauty," Darcy remarked softly.

"The twilight?" Elizabeth sighed. "No, it gets better and better every time."

Darcy took her hand and brought it to his lips. Looking into her eyes, he said softly, "That it does."

Finis

A special thank you to Sara Angelini, Debbie Styne, Brandy Scott, Amy Johnson, and Debra Anne Watson for their help in the making of this story. Without you, this would be little more than an unfinished document abandoned on my hard drive.

Thank you to the girls at GeorgiaGirlsRock, official and honorary—in particular to Pat, Lorie, Theresa, and Crystal who have been some of the dearest friends I have ever known.

Another thank you goes to everyone who loved Jane Austen's novels so much they could not bear to see them to end.

To David, my love, who believes in me when I forget to believe in myself.

Casey Childers is a native of Atlanta Georgia, and has been a lover of literature and all things Austen throughout her life. She offers this piece as a humble offering in homage to whom she considers the greatest novelist of all time.

Made in the USA
Lexington, KY
22 April 2010